Lost in London

Also by Cindy Callaghan
Just Add Magic

Lost in London

CINDY CALLAGHAN

Aladdin M!X
New York London Toronto Sydney New Delhi

This book is a work of fiction. Any references to historical events, real people, or real places are used fictitiously. Other names, characters, places, and events are products of the author's imagination, and any resemblance to actual events or places or persons, living or dead, is entirely coincidental.

ALADDIN M!X
Simon & Schuster Children's Publishing Division
1230 Avenue of the Americas, New York, NY 10020
First Aladdin M!X edition October 2013
Text copyright © 2013 by Cindy Callaghan
Cover illustration copyright © 2013 by Annabelle Metayer
Cover design by Jessica Handelman
All rights reserved, including the right of reproduction in whole or in part in any form.
ALADDIN is a trademark of Simon & Schuster, Inc., and related logo is a registered trademark of Simon & Schuster, Inc.
ALADDIN M!X and related logo are registered trademarks of Simon & Schuster, Inc.
For information about special discounts for bulk purchases, please contact Simon & Schuster Special Sales at 1-866-506-1949 or business@simonandschuster.com.
The Simon & Schuster Speakers Bureau can bring authors to your live event. For more information or to book an event contact the Simon & Schuster Speakers Bureau at 1-866-248-3049 or visit our website at www.simonspeakers.com.
Interior design by Hilary Zarycky
The text of this book was set in ITC Berkeley Oldstyle.
Manufactured in the United States of America 0116 OFF
10 9
Library of Congress Control Number 2013939119
ISBN 978-1-4424-6653-1 (pbk)
ISBN 978-1-4424-6654-8 (eBook)

This book, and really everything, is dedicated to
Ellie, Evan, and Happy.

Acknowledgments

There are so many very special people I would like to thank:

I am very lucky to be part of two critique groups. Both helped me shape this book. To the WIPs: Gale, Carolee, Josette, Jane, Chris, and Shannon, the last nine years have flown by. You're awesome. To the Northern Delaware Sisters in Crime group: John, KB, Jane, June, Chris, Jacqui, Susan, Kathleen, and Pat, thanks for feedback.

Mom and Dad: Thanks for your continued confidence in me and for your endless support.

To my nieces and nephews: Mikayla, Anna, John, Christopher, Sean, Keelen, Lauren, Nikki, Taylor, Danny, Kelsey, and Shawn. Thanks for all the great material. You're a fun bunch.

To Sue, Mark, and in-laws and out-laws who never fail to ask me, "How's the writing going?" Thank you for your interest and endless ideas.

To my friends, near and far, old and new: You inspire me!

To my agent, Mandy Hubbard: "Thank you" doesn't seem like enough for making my dream career a reality. I appreciate your confidence in me.

To my editor, Alyson Heller, and the whole team at Simon & Schuster: You're a class act! Thanks for everything.

To Kevin: Thank you for supporting my dream career. You're a great partner.

To my readers: None of this works without you. Thank you for reading and for inviting me to your schools, libraries, and book clubs. I love getting your e-mails and letters. I hope you love *Lost in London* as much as *Just Add Magic*.

Lost in London

1

The flyer in my hand said it was a one-week student program in London—as in the most exciting city in Europe. I needed something exciting, anything other than what was called "my life."

Everybody has a "thing." Some people are good at sports, or music, or are popular, or are at the bottom of the social ladder.

Except me. I didn't have a thing. Translation? I was a positively ordinary thirteen-year-old girl who led a boring life. Consider my life's report card:

- I lived in a regular old town without a palm tree, igloo, or palace (Wilmington, Delaware) = blah.
- I didn't do any sports or clubs = yawn.
- I wasn't allowed to wear makeup, ride my bike without a helmet, go to R movies, or attend boy-girl dances = lame.
- I lived next door to my school, where my dad worked = annoying.
- Worst of all, I'd never done anything exciting. When I explained this to my parents, they brought up my trip with the Girl Scouts last year. I didn't think that should count, because it was only two nights and my mom was there. It was totally Dullsville. (I dropped out of Girl Scouts right after.)

This school-sponsored trip was like a miracle opportunity sent directly to me, Jordan Jacoby. *What could be more exciting than London?* (Paris, possibly, but that doesn't matter right now.) I wanted to go to London to become worldly by traveling around that amazing city and soaking in its history and culture.

There was just one problem. Kind of a biggie. My parents.

I studied the London program information on my short walk home from school—across the football field, through a gate, along a short path, and onto the sidewalk that led to my house. My dad was a little ways behind me, walking home too.

Let me give you some advice if your parents ever consider working at your school:

Talk them out of it.

Sabotage the interview.

Recruit someone else for the job.

Do whatever it takes for them to work anywhere other than at your school. Seriously, anywhere. And if they somehow manage to get the job, beg them to change their name and pretend they don't know you.

I love my dad, but walking to and from school with him every day, and seeing him lurk in the hallways, sucked any possible element of fun from my middle-school existence. I couldn't so much as draw on my sneaker with a permanent marker, or talk to a boy, without getting "the look." The you-and-I-both-know-you-shouldn't-be-doing-that look.

Ah, London.

I wanted this trip.

"What are you reading?" Dad walked faster to catch up with me.

"About the school-sponsored trip to London this year. I really, really want to go."

He immediately harrumphed, but I didn't let that stop me. This was going to take persistence. And I could be seriously persistent.

The conversation about the trip went on all afternoon and into dinner. "There has got to be more to the world than Wilmington, Delaware. I've never done anything or gone anywhere."

"Now, that's just not true," Mom said. "You went away overnight to Girl Scout camp. Remember that?"

Oh, yeah. Did I ever.

I tried: "Oh, come on. You never let me do anything fun. And it's only five days."

Then I went to: "We live in an American-centric society. Isn't it important for me to broaden my horizons?" (I'd gotten that from the flyer.)

I added: "I have the assignment all planned out. It's going to be a photo montage of sights with narration. I promise I'll get an A, or maybe an A-minus, on it and I'll weed all summer long to pay you back for the trip."

Finally I went with: "It will be an experience that I will remember for the rest of my life!"

My mom talked about me staying with an old friend of hers who had a stepdaughter about my age. This made me think she was seriously considering it. Then she started talking about the dangers of a foreign city—drugs, kidnapping—and the cost of the trip. It wasn't looking good.

Then—I don't know what happened exactly—but at that moment, on Marsh Road in Wilmington, Delaware, a miracle occurred. They said YES!

I was going to embark on a journey called the De-bored-ification of Jordan Jacoby.

Only, I had no idea how de-bored-ified my life was about to become.

2

A few weeks later I got off my first plane ever. My eyes felt like they'd been dusted with sand. I followed signs toward Customs. There were lots of signs, and my mind wasn't working clearly, so I ended up just following a lady who had been on my flight and hoped that she wasn't connecting to Africa.

After I waited in a line, a customs officer stamped my passport: ENGLAND!

It was official.

I had arrived.

I looked for someone who matched Caroline Littleton's online picture. Instead I found a tall man in a simple black suit holding a sign, JORDAN JACOBY.

"I'm Jordan," I told him.

"Welcome to London. I'm Liam. Shall we get your bags and proceed to the manor house?"

"Sure," I said, half-excited to be taken to the "manor house" by a chauffeur, and half-bummed that Caroline hadn't met me at the airport herself.

"Very well. Off we go." His accent was so sophisticated. I loved it.

I followed him to the luggage claim and then outside, where he opened the back door of a black car with a rounded roof. The first thing I noticed was that the steering wheel was on the wrong side. Well, maybe it wasn't wrong if you lived in London, but it was opposite from the US. I'd never been driven like this, like, *by a driver*. Carpooling didn't even compare.

I wouldn't see the airport again for five days. As far as programs abroad went, this one was short, over spring break. The only requirement was to return with the assignment—a summary of my trip. My grandparents had gotten me a new phone with a really good camera (for pictures and videos) just for the trip. (*Yay for grandparents!*)

My parents had agreed that I had to get an A or A-minus on the presentation, and I would spend the summer pulling weeds to pay for the trip. It wasn't the dandelions-in-grass kind of weeding. It was the sweat-and-dirt-and-worms-and-poison-ivy kind. They also gave me some money and an emergency credit card. If I charged anything to the card that wasn't a true emergency, I'd pay it off by spreading fertilizer around our tomatoes. You know what's in fertilizer? It rhymes with "droop."

We drove through London on the wrong side of the road; well, maybe not wrong. I videoed or photographed everything—buildings, street signs, double-decker tour buses, cafés, stores. There was no predicting what I'd need when I edited the montage. And I really wanted it to be good—well, at least A-minus good so that I wouldn't have to do more yard work.

I was going to stay with a friend of my mom's—a sorority sister who she really liked but hadn't seen in years. She was Caroline's stepmom (well, "mum," I suppose). They had discussed the itinerary. It was going to be an amazing week, like palaces-castles-abbeys-gardens-cathedrals amazing. I was going to see and do everything, absolutely everything, and return to Wilmington as a totally different person!

I wondered if Caroline and I would possibly have

time to sleep, because as much as I wanted to see London and begin the process of changing my life from boring to well traveled, I also really needed a power nap. I'd stayed up all night watching movies on the plane.

BTW, there were several movies to choose from, and I picked one that was PG-13.

"First time in England?" Liam asked.

"Yup! I've never been anywhere." This was true if you didn't count Girl Scouts, which I didn't.

"Nowhere, Miss Jordan? Well, you've chosen the best city in the world. I've lived here my entire life." He smiled at me in the rearview mirror, showing a mouthful of crooked teeth. "We should be at the Littletons' house in a few moments."

The city became country. It looked like it'd recently rained. Sections of damp grass glistened in the sun. Liam pulled into a long driveway to a very large Tudor-style house. Ivy clung to its frame; moss padded the roof's tiles. It was fairy-tale perfect, just like I'd hoped it would be.

I didn't have much information about Caroline. My mom had never actually met her. Her Facebook page made her sound so . . . so . . . so worldly. She rode horses, and liked music, shopping, and going out in London with her friends. She was everything I wanted to be. I knew already that we were going to be BFFs, just like our moms.

Liam stopped the car, and I opened the door and got out. The look on his face as he came around the trunk said I should've waited, but I didn't get back in. I was going to walk up to the house, but decided to wait for him to get my bags—well, bag. I only had one suitcase. I flung my backpack over one shoulder and followed Liam to the front door. He opened it and ushered me inside.

I expected Caroline and her parents to be waiting excitedly for me, maybe with balloons, but the house was silent. And beautiful. The walls were trimmed with dark woodwork. Art and mirrors hung on the walls; every surface held a vase of fresh-cut flowers. The room smelled like springtime but a little damp, too, like some of last night's rain had seeped in through the old cracks. This was the closest thing to a palace I'd ever been in. And hopefully in a few short hours I'd be hanging out in London, learning about kings and queens and basically becoming less boring every minute.

Liam led me to a kitchen and waved me to sit at the table. "Energizer?"

I was proud of myself because I knew he meant OJ. The stewardess on the plane had offered it to me. I'd felt dumb when I'd asked her what it was, but now I knew.

"Sure. Thanks. Um, where's Caroline?"

He looked at the clock. "She should be down soon. Mister has already left for work, and Mrs. Littleton—" A Mini Cooper zipped into the driveway. "Oh, there she is."

Through the window I saw a petite woman in yoga clothes run to the front door. "You're here!" she said with the perkiness I'd hoped for. "Let me look atcha." She had an accent like she was from Tennessee or Louisiana that didn't fit with this house or London. "You look just like your mama. Lord, seeing you makes me miss her. How is she?"

"She's fine."

"Well, let's get you some breakfast." She asked Liam, "Where's Caroline?"

"Still in bed, I suspect, madam."

"That child. I told her to go with you to the airport." She smiled at me. "I'm sorry she didn't greet you. She just doesn't understand how much fun y'all are gonna have. I've told her this will be a good experience for her, too, but she's very focused on her friends. I'm sure you understand."

I nodded like I did, but I wasn't so sure. I thought she'd just told me that Caroline wasn't excited that I was here.

"I always wished that I'd had more experiences with

different kinds of people when I was thirteen, and I just want that for her."

Liam fixed me a small bowl of berries and added a dollop of white cream, which I assumed was yogurt, but it tasted more like sour cream, so I picked around it to get to the berries. As I started to eat, Liam quietly left the room.

A minute later a girl in pj's with bed head, a sleep mask pushed up to her forehead, and eyes barely open came in and picked up the orange juice that Liam had just poured for me.

I hopped out of my chair, ready to grab her in a totally huge, psyched-to-be-here hug.

She sipped again before opening her eyes and finding me a few inches from her face. "Oh my," she said. Her eyes opened wider. "You must be . . . Jordan?"

"Here I am!" I tossed my arms into the air.

"Yes, you are," she said. And she looked at me from sneakers to ponytail. Her flat expression told me that she wasn't seeing anything she liked, probably because everything was boring. I casually let the smile drain from my face. She sipped the orange juice again.

An awkward silence blew through the kitchen, during which I sat back down and scooped another berry into my mouth. "I'm so excited to be here, like

Christmas-morning-excited. I mean, it's London! A city of castles, real princesses, and knights jousting till death," I said. Then I caught my own zealousness and calmly asked, "What do you want to do today?"

Mrs. Littleton fanned out a handful of brochures that she'd taken out of a drawer. "Here's a load of information about all the places that your mama and I discussed. Y'all can look through to give you ideas of stuff to do. Liam can take you where you want to go, or you can take the train into the city."

"You aren't coming?" I asked. My mom had been pretty clear that Mrs. Littleton would accompany us.

"No," Caroline said. "I explained to her that we can get along quite well on our own. I go all around the city on my own all the time."

Mrs. Littleton said, "Now, not so fast. I want to know where y'all are at." She addressed Caroline, "So call me and text me. It's not like you'll just be going anywhere you want without telling me." Then she faced me again. "You okay with that?"

Caroline was behind her stepmother's back, mocking her by making a mouth with her fingers and thumb. She opened and closed them in a comical way, and I had to chew on my lip to keep from laughing out loud.

I nodded that I was good with that, but I knew my

parents would NOT be . . . if they knew, which they wouldn't, because I wasn't going to tell them.

When Mrs. Littleton turned, Caroline snapped her hand down. "All right," she said. "Then everything is bril." I was pretty sure that was short for "brilliant." I couldn't wait to use that word. Maybe I could mention how bril the energizer was?

"Super," Mrs. Littleton said. "I just know you two are gonna be—what do you kids say? BFFs! That's it. I'm gonna shower. I'll see y'all later. Have fun."

Caroline fixed herself a bowl of berries and swiped the brochures right into the trash. "I'll get dressed. I was thinking we'd go shopping, to Daphne's, of course. I'll be down in a wee bit." She left the kitchen with her berries, but then poked her head back in. "By the way, knights don't actually joust till death anymore, and castles are a bit old and damp." She left.

I didn't think I'd made a very good first impression. And I was really bummed that she wasn't psyched that I was here. I mean, she'd been *asleep*! Maybe she'd get to know me better while we shopped and then she'd like me. I had to work on my coolness factor at the store or mall. And after shopping, we could start on the sights for my montage.

I reached into the trash can for the brochures. Then

Caroline stuck her head in for the second time. I pretended like I wasn't picking in the garbage. "You might want to change and get freshened up before we go," she said. "Liam can show you to your room and give you a call when we're ready to go."

She left me in the kitchen, alone.

3

I managed to find Liam, who showed me to an incredible guest room: all cream-colored with a four-poster bed with a frilly canopy. French doors opened out to a balcony overlooking a field fit for horses trotting in from a fox hunt.

The attached bathroom was marble and silver. I took a quick shower and changed into what I hoped was an appropriate shopping outfit: jeans and turtleneck with a fleece vest.

I looked in the mirror. Hmmmm. Not awful, but not really "London."

Shopping could be exactly what I needed to help me move out of Dullsville, although money could be a problem. I'd budgeted one hundred dollars per day. When I'd transferred the currency, it had felt like I had a lot less money. *Can I afford to shop?*

The way Caroline looked—the way this house looked—money was no object. It was totally crazy to think that I was going to spend a whole week in this mansion!

I looked through my bag and found a scarf that I'd brought in case it got cold. I added it and reassessed. Not much better. Glancing at my reflection in an antique mirror, I decided this was an emergency. A fashion emergency, that is. I twisted around in the mirror, pouting my lips at the girl staring back at me.

Jordan, you desperately need to go shopping.

I brushed my hair and tousled it with my fingers to make it bouncy and full, but it still looked blah. Not "bad" blah, like "ordinary" blah.

I studied my map of London while waiting to be *fetched*. People here totally said "fetched," right? Eventually Liam came to the guest room door. "Miss Jordan? Ready to go shopping?"

I snapped up. "Yup!" I took a second to re-fluff my hair and straighten my fleece vest.

Liam led me to the front door, his shiny shoes tapping on the gleaming hardwood floors. I let out a yawn and tried to shake the fuzz out of my head. I could easily sleep until dinner . . . maybe until dinner tomorrow. And I was hungry, like double-burger-fries-and-a-shake hungry.

Caroline stood by the car talking on her cell phone. She was way more dressed up than me: boots like I'd seen only in a magazine—they went up to her knees—and a skirt that defined the word "mini." I practically drooled over her chunky bracelets. I couldn't see her eyes under bejeweled sunglasses—odd, since it had turned cloudy—but I suspected she wore makeup to match her red lipstick. She looked like she could be fifteen easily. Suddenly even my cute scarf felt worse than drab.

It looked like Caroline would know exactly what I needed to transform. I wondered if I could get that look, if she could teach me to be glamorous.

Caroline clapped her phone shut. "Liam!" she called, and turned to see us. "Oh, there you are." She gave me an extra look over the top of her glasses but didn't comment. "Sam, Gordo, and Ellie are meeting us at Daphne's."

Liam held the car door open, and I got into the back like I'd had a driver all my life. Caroline propped the sunglasses on her head. I was right—eye makeup. "Is Daphne one of your friends?"

"Are you serious? Daphne isn't a *who*. It's a *what*. And it's the most crackin' *what* to shop at in all of London. You wanted to see the sights." She checked her lipstick in a compact mirror. "And, trust me, Daphne's is quite a sight. People from all over Europe, Asia, the Middle East, and even from the other side of the pond come to London to shop at Daphne's. You're going to love it. First stop, lattes. *Oui?*"

"*Oui,*" I said, like I had lattes and drizzled French words like "*oui*" into my conversations all the time.

Looking out of the window, feeling a little self-conscious in my basic Old Navy clothes, I felt my mood improve as we drove over the London Bridge . . . THE actual London Bridge. The one the song is about. Then we passed the Marble Arch, and Madame Tussauds—all places I was dying to see. I couldn't wait to visit them all. I snapped picture after picture. It started raining heavily, like nor'easter-heavy raining. I doubted that they called them nor'easters here.

"It's supposed to storm quite hard today," Liam said. "That's why they call it Rainy London."

He pulled over. I looked for a store. "Where is it?" I asked.

Caroline said, "You're next to it."

I squinted. "All I see is this big hotel."

"That's not a hotel. That's eighteen floors of blooming shopping perfection."

"Eighteen? That's a lot of floors," I said, craning my neck to see to the top.

"Yes. And in order to get through all of them, we're going to need some energy in the form of caffeine. So, let the lattes begin!"

"*Oui,*" I experimented. I didn't get a funny look from Caroline, so I think I used it right. *Yay, me!*

I thanked Liam and followed Caroline, like a puppy, through the downpour into the store. I noticed I wasn't the only puppy, but the others were riding into Daphne's inside designer handbags. People toted their pooches along with them. If I were taking notes, I would've definitely written that down.

I hiked my backpack onto my shoulder. I felt a little guilty to be at a big Macy's instead of exploring the sights of London, but there would be plenty of time for that after I shopped. And, really, this little shopping trip was vitally important to the new me.

I glanced at the store directory—a holographic map projected onto a humungous wall. It showed everything that could be found on the eighteen floors, from sun hats to snowshoes, and everything imaginable in between. Every brand I had ever heard of and hundreds—no, thousands—that I hadn't, crowded the directory. The map was in English, French, Spanish, and symbols that I thought might be Arabic. It looked like everything ever made in the world was in this store.

This could be more than a little shopping trip; this might be a complete fashion transformation, even if that meant a summer of shoveling poop.

4

I trailed after Caroline through what seemed like department after department of purses.

"We can come back and you can look for a purse later. You need one." Apparently my L.L.Bean backpack didn't cut it. "But I want to find my mates first. You'll love them. I'm sure Ellie will want to get a mani at the salon here." A mani? I'd never had one.

Salon, hmmm . . . what if I get my hair trimmed? Maybe Caroline could look through those hair books with me and help me pick out a new do?

"Do you know all of them?" I asked. "The floors, I mean?"

"Oh, yes. I've been coming here since I was in my gingham plaid pram."

"What's a *pram*? Like a shirt?"

"Uh, no." I think she rolled her eyes. "It's a buggy, a baby stroller."

She spoke English, but it was like a totally different language. I thought about my baby cousin and decided that the next time I saw her, I was going to use the word "pram."

Caroline walked toward a giant copper cappuccino machine that sat behind a high counter. Three people were waiting for us—a girl and two guys. They offered Caroline hugs, and the girls oohed and aahed about Caroline's sunglasses. Apparently, they were something special.

I waited for her to introduce me. For a second I thought she'd forgotten that I was there, but then she said, "This is Jordan. She's from the States and needed a place to stay, so she's living with us for the week."

Needed a place to stay?

"Actually it's like a study abroad program," I said. "I see the sights with Caroline and her family, and when I get back, I'll do a report about it for school."

"Well, that's exciting," Caroline said like she didn't mean it. "A report for school?"

Did those totally lame words just come out of my mouth? "Actually, I was going to do a photo and video montage of my trip and narrate over it." Her expression said that this didn't impress her either.

A boy dressed just about as well as Caroline (leather ankle boots, blazer over a cashmere turtleneck) said, "At least you'll have something totally brilliant to report—Daphne's. People bite off their arm to come here. You should find plenty to montage—eighteen floors' worth. Can you believe it, eighteen? I know, it's unbelievable, eh?" He stretched out his hand. "I'm Gordo."

"Hi," I said. "I guess you know who I am." I tried to rebound from "school report." "This is bril. I can't wait to shop. Very bril." Okay, maybe one too many "brils," but it was progress.

"Ooh, I love your accent . . . ," Caroline's friend with double-pierced ears and spiky hair said. "It's so . . . different."

"Thanks," I said, unsure if she really meant it as a compliment.

"Where are you from?" she asked.

"Wilmington," I said.

"Is that near Los Angeles?"

"Um, yup. It's near LA." Crap, I was reinventing myself as a liar. "Kinda, sorta near it."

"I'm Ellie with an *i-e*," said Spiky Hair. "I'm changing from a *y*. So, it's kind of a big deal."

"Interesting," I said, and I really thought it was. Maybe I'd change the spelling of my name. "How's that working for you?"

"So far it's like a bomb. I feel like a new person already. Which I guess I kind of am. You know, with the *i-e* and everything."

"Yup." I mentally considered this. *Jordan Jacoby . . . Jor? Jor Jack? J Jack? J.J.?* "My friends call me J.J.," I said quietly to test it with Ellie and see if the new name was okay.

"J.J.," Ellie said as if trying it out. "I like it."

Yay! I did too. In fact, it felt like a bomb. Like a whole-big-new-image bomb.

Gordo stopped gushing over Caroline's clothes long enough to order a skinny latte. "Fancy one?"

"Sure. Thanks. I'd fancy one." (I'd just said "fancy.") I'd heard people order coffee drinks whose names went on for half an hour . . . *A double mocha joka jerky over ice with a peppermint twist and a Kansas City pickle on the side.* "Whatever you're having."

"You got it, baby doll," Gordo said as he moved up in line.

Baby doll? I was gonna use that one at home too.

Gordo asked, "So, what's your story, J.J.?"

It took me half a second to realize he was talking to me. I was J.J. "Oh, you know, the usual. Regular thirteen-year-old girl." Little did Gordo know that "regular" was an exaggeration.

"What do you like to do?" he asked.

"You know, stuff. Girl stuff."

"Like regular thirteen-year-old girl stuff?"

"Exactly," I said, laughing.

"I see. So, you're not like an undercover secret agent or something? Or a famous movie star pretending to be an ordinary girl to get away from the paparazzi?"

"I'm positive."

Gordo's questions were interrupted when he ordered coffee.

The other guy with them had only looked in the cases of gourmet food. He bought a large bag of jelly beans. "I'm Sam. And for the record, I'm here for the candy, not the shopping." Whether you were in America or England, there was one word to describe Sam, and that word was "cute." He had rock-star blond hair that was longish in the front and buzzed in the back.

"Candy?"

"Okay," Sam said. "You got me." He pushed the long-ish part of his hair out of his eyes. "I like the pastries, too. I'm in search of a lemon tart from Lively's. It's just over there a bit, around the bend. When it's all clear, I'll get one."

Then he put his index finger and pinkie to his ear and mouth, like a phone. "Ring, bring!" he said. "Hello?" Then he said in a different voice, like it was the person on the other end of the phone talking, "Hi, this is the Truth Society calling. We just heard you tell a lie." And then he said, "Okay, you got me. I'll get at least two lemon tarts." The hand-phone disappeared.

"Um, okay," I said, not sure how to react to this strangeness. "Why do you have to wait for the all clear?"

Ellie picked up her coffee cup and turned around as she slid a bright pink straw through the little hole in the lid. "Because of Sebastian Lively. Lively is with a y. He works there for his dad. They own Lively's bakery in town. It's so popular that Daphne's asked them to open a counter here. And he works at it. Anyway, Sebastian is both annoying and evil. He hates us—well, mostly Caroline—because she told everyone he was half-midget and born in a circus."

"I had meant it to be funny," Caroline defended

herself. "Turns out he's a half midget with no sense of humor."

Ellie laughed a little too hard. Caroline gave a very subtle head shake that told everyone that the laugh annoyed her. Ellie must've caught on, because she stopped and quickly added, "Sorry."

"Because Sebastian hates Caroline, he automatically hates us, too. So, it's not safe to eat his tarts," Sam said. "Even though Sebastian is a royal jerk—and I do mean *royal*, because he claims that somewhere in his lineage he has royal blood—his family's bakery is still the best."

"The best," Gordo confirmed.

Ellie continued, "Gordo convinced Sam that when Sebastian sees us coming, he spits in the lemon tarts."

"Seriously?" I asked. *Ew.*

"Totally serious." Gordo handed me a big cup that felt light, like it was only half-full. "Sebastian has quite a deviously creative mind."

I sipped the warm coffee drink and refrained from making a yuck-face, because if these cool kids drank lattes, then so could I.

I watched as Gordo used silver tongs to add brown sugar cubes to his drink. When he handed me the tongs, I did the same. The brown sugar dissolved, and I sipped it again. It was better. Good, actually. I liked holding this tall cup with a cardboard protector sleeve on it. The first thing I was going to do when I got home was go to Cup O' Joes and order a latte. My friend Darbie from home would be so impressed.

Caroline and Ellie joined us with their matching icy tan drinks. The straws had red lipstick rings at the top. I wanted to buy a tube of lipstick. I knew the cherry-flavored ChapStick in my backpack didn't make a ring like that.

"Shall we shop?" Caroline asked.

"Yes!" Ellie and Gordo said in unison. Sam ate a jelly bean.

Caroline looked at her watch. "Five and a half hours till closing."

I'd never shopped for five and a half hours! "Power-shopping" had a whole new meaning here.

"Why don't you go on ahead," Sam said. "J.J. looks like she wants a lemon tart."

Gordo narrowed his eyes at Sam. "Be careful." Then he looked at our group, which was about to split up. "Duli for dinner at seven?"

Caroline and Ellie nodded and slurped with their straws.

"Okay," said Ellie. "But for the record I have no respect for a place that ends with an *i*. It's like they couldn't decide between the *i-e* or the *y*. No respect at all."

Gordo whispered to Sam, "Duli is on the fifth floor behind the Persian rugs."

"Thanks. I can read a store map," Sam whispered back.

To me Gordo said, "Don't fill up on lemon tarts. There's lots of fish and chips to ingest. Cheers!"

"Cheers!" I echoed back. Fish and chips didn't sound good to me. I stuck with the usual stuff like burgers (no cheese), spaghetti (no sauce), and pretzels.

When they left, Sam said, "Don't like fish and chips, eh?"

"I love 'em. I can't wait for a dish of fish," I lied again. The un-boring of Jordan Jacoby would now include new foods too!

I followed him across the pretty lacquered floors, and he glanced back at me as we went deeper into the store. "You didn't look like you wanted to shop."

"I didn't?" *Of course I want to shop. How am I going to get a new look without shopping?*

"It's a gift I have. Like a sixth sense. Freaky, eh?" He grinned, and I realized he had dimples, really cute dimples.

"A little, I guess. But maybe it's not working well today, because I kinda would like to shop."

"Huh? Really? Strange. It's never not worked before. You don't look like a shopper."

I hope the translation of that didn't mean: "That ugly outfit looks like a hand-me-down."

I smelled it before I could see it: cinnamon and chocolate, cakes and pies baking. The scent entranced me and drew me deeper into the store. But the sight was even better.

It was an absolutely incredible scene, like Willy Wonka incredible. The Hall of Gourmets (kind of like a fancy food court, inside Daphne's) was dedicated solely to sweets. The display went way beyond candy to every type of baked treat you could imagine. A kiosk of bouquets made of cookies stood in the center; another kiosk specialized in cakes stacked five layers high. One cake was a replica of the store, with incredible detail right down to the brick front and windows showcasing dresses, sporting equipment, and toys. One area was floor to ceiling tubes of gummies. A tall ladder on wheels held a man who filled the tubes from the tops. Kids opened the bottom and let the candy pieces fall into their bags.

At the end of the hall I saw letters in glittery lights: Lively's.

It took me a minute to absorb the variety of desserts

around me, during which I lost sight of Sam. I turned in every direction but couldn't find him in his red long-sleeved oxford, untucked from his baggy jeans.

Someone tugged on my backpack, and I twisted around, then finally looked down. Sam was crouched down behind a potted plant.

5

"What are you doing?" I whispered to Sam.

"Hiding from Sebastian. He's there, working the counters. The short redheaded kid in the pink apron. If he sees me, I'm a goner."

I couldn't decide if it was better to crouch down or just keep talking, because it probably looked like I was chatting up a giant fern. "Goner? Really?"

"Fine, the Drama Police called, and they said maybe I'm not a goner, but I won't get a tart, which is pretty much the same thing. My blood sugar is low."

"Do you even know what low blood sugar is?" I didn't mention that he'd just pounded a ton of jelly beans.

"No. But mine is probably low, and that can't be a good thing."

Having grandparents who were diabetic, I knew what blood sugar was, but I didn't see the point in explaining it. I looked at Lively's. "So that short guy is Sebastian?"

"Yes. That's the evil bloke."

Sebastian waited on customers, rung them up, and wished them a nice day. "He looks harmless enough."

"Don't be fooled, J.J." Sam said.

I liked the sound of my new name. "I'll get you your tart," I offered. He was right. He was a British drama king hiding behind a potted plant in the Hall of Gourmets.

He said, "I couldn't ask you to do that, but it's a good idea. He won't know you."

I marched toward the line. When Sebastian came to take my order, he was very polite. "Two lemon tarts, please. Actually, make it three." I remembered that Sam wanted two.

He got me the tarts in a totally non-evil way. He used a square of waxy paper to pull them out of the glass case. When he turned to the counter to grab a box, my view was obstructed for a sec. Then he appeared with the box wrapped in red string. I paid for the tarts with some English coins.

Then Sebastian leaned over the counter to hand me my change. He motioned me closer. I leaned in.

"Tell Sam I can see him, eh?" he said, and gave me a totally evil grin.

My eyebrows shot up. I turned toward Sam and realized the potted plant was in front of a big mirror. He wasn't hidden at all.

"Nice try," Sebastian added as I walked away.

I pushed out a smile, my cheeks red from embarrassment. When I got back to Sam, I held up the box. "Success."

He took it.

I added, "Oh, and Sebastian says hi."

"Blast it! He saw me?"

"Afraid so."

He slid his butt onto the ground, blew the long pieces of blond hair out of his face, and rested his head against the pot. He held up the box. "Just take them away so I'm not tempted."

I took the box.

He said, "Do it."

"Do what?"

"Throw it away."

"Really?" I scowled. I'm pretty sure I paid at least ten bucks for those things. "That's such a waste."

"Rubbish! That's what this is! We'll come back later when he's gone. But I can't risk it . . . You know, the spit." He kind of gagged like the thought of Sebastian's saliva made him almost puke. I didn't like the idea myself.

I threw away the white box. Total bummer, since I was *starving*. Now I'd have to wait until seven o'clock for fish and chips.

He asked, "Wanna go for a walk or something?"

What I really wanted to do was find Caroline and get started on my new look before we toured the city.

I was going to see and do absolutely everything in a new outfit! I didn't care if I didn't sleep for five days. . . . Oh, the thought of sleep reminded me how tired I was. I really needed to sleep. I also really needed a snack.

"Bring! Bring!" Sam said, interrupting my thoughts. "Anybody home?"

I snapped to attention. "A walk sounds good." My stomach growled. "But I think I'm going to get a cookie."

"You'd better get it from over there. They don't . . . you know." He pretended like he was spitting.

I went to the place with the cookie bouquets and got a big sugar cookie and ate it in three bites.

"Wow," Sam said. He held up his hand with a finger toward his mouth and another toward his ear like a pretend phone. "This is the Hungry Company. Is J.J. there?" He held his hand toward me. "It's for you."

I giggled a little bit. I didn't actually understand the phone thing, but it was funny. I wanted to get to know Sam better. He was goofy, but not in a dorky way. And even a dull American could see he was very good-looking.

"British girls are all itsy-bitsy about their bites of tiny sandwiches. It's so unrealistic. If you're hungry, you're hungry." Then he added, "Let's go. If you've never been here, there's some cool stuff I can show you. Like the Hole."

6

"There's a hole?"

"Well, that's what they call it. It's more like a lift shaft without the lift," he said.

Maybe "pram" wasn't in my pre-trip homework, but I knew that "lift" was an elevator, so that gave me a decent picture.

When we stood at the bottom of the Hole and looked up eighteen floors, I understood what he was trying to explain. It *was* like an elevator shaft, but instead of being surrounded by walls, it was surrounded by escalators that made a square frame. Some department must've been giving away balloons, because a few floated up.

"This is all one store?"

"Yup. One big store that takes up a city block."

Sam hopped on the up escalator.

We rode up one story and stopped on the landing. A glass display case showed what was on that floor. This floor was Toys, so the windows on the landing were decorated with games, puzzles, stuffed animals, remote control planes, and electric cars. Music trickled out from inside the toy department, and a line of kids snaked out the door.

"Every few floors there's something for kids to do while their parents shop. My little sister loves to come with my mom to play dress-up in the Formal Wear Department."

The next floor was Cosmetics and Jewelry, where we could smell the faint scents of various perfumes. The mannequins in the windows were drenched in necklaces and bracelets.

Hmmm . . . maybe my makeover can start on this floor?

Eventually we passed Persian rugs, so I knew that was where we were having dinner. As we walked, I scanned the crowd. People of every color and nationality I could imagine were browsing the store: women with black shrouds over their heads that only allowed a crack for their eyes, men with long black beards and furry sideburns, people with pale white skin to very dark brown skin and black hair.

"What do you think?" Sam asked as we went up another level.

Daphne's wasn't the ginormous London Eye Ferris wheel that overlooked the Thames River (which was one of the things I really wanted to do this week), but I had to admit, it was pretty amazing. "It's definitely bigger than I thought it would be. I don't know of any place quite like it in the US. We have big department stores like Bloomingdale's and Saks Fifth Avenue. It's like this place ate those stores *and* a carnival. Is there anything it doesn't have?"

"A planetarium, a racetrack, and an ice rink. They're working on a cinema and a bowling alley."

I thought he was kidding me, but he didn't laugh. "Seriously," he said. "And a helicopter pad on the roof for people traveling from really far. Later this year they'll let people bungee from off the side of the building."

I narrowed my eyes.

He grinned. "Okay, you got me. I made that one up. Don't call the Exaggeration Patrol. But the others are true, and if I made a suggestion about the bungee, I bet they'd make that happen too."

"Maybe you should."

"Maybe I will," he said, playfully pushing my shoulder.

"We should find Caroline," I suggested.

"Good idea," Sam said. "Let's round up the gang and play a game of Slip Away."

7

"What's Slip Away?" I asked.

"We use the whole store. One group flees and the other searches. Every fifteen minutes the flee-ers text the searchers a clue about where they're hiding."

"It sounds like hide-and-seek."

"Hide-and-seek is for tots. This is way more."

Sam clicked at his phone, which he called a "mobile" (with a long *i*, so it rhymed with "pile"), as we approached the landing of Formal Wear and Kids' Dress-Up Department on the tenth floor.

"They're on their way," he said.

A minute later the golden double doors of an elevator opened. Out walked Caroline, carrying multiple big white shopping bags with the Daphne's logo. Ellie and Gordo came out behind her, each also carrying a bag or two.

Did I miss the shopping?

"Game on?" Gordo asked. His hair had been gelled up like a rock star's, and I think he'd put on eyeliner. They'd gone to the salon! I *had* missed it.

Sam nodded and gave his friend a fist bump.

"Oh, I don't know," said Ellie, examining her cuticles. "I was hoping for a manicure." *Oh, me too!* Maybe I could go home with long elegant nails.

Gordo said, "You can get a mani any day. In fact, I'll come back with you tomorrow if you want."

"Okay, then I'm in," she said.

Caroline sighed. "Fine. But I'll need to find a locker."

Gordo took her bags from her hands. "I'll take care of that for you. There's some by the loo." He disappeared down a hallway with a restroom sign.

"What are the teams?" Ellie asked. "Last time I fleed and this time I want to search. I could be like the captain of the searchers."

"Let's do the coin method," Sam said. "It's the most fair."

Gordo reappeared. "Good plan."

Sam reached into the pocket of his baggy jeans and handed a coin to everyone. "Odd years are searchers. Even years are flee-ers."

I took the coin Sam gave me and looked at the date: 1970. "Even," I said.

"Odd," said Gordo and Ellie. They moved next to each other.

"Even," Sam said.

Caroline didn't say anything but moved to our even team.

"It's three versus two." Sam, Caroline, and I were going to hide.

Gordo said, "You better run. You only have two minutes."

Sam took off.

"I love to search. You guys better watch out," Ellie called after us. "I'm coming after you!"

Caroline tried to keep up with Sam and me, but with her high-heeled boots, running didn't come easily. I almost crashed into a group of women wearing colorful belly dancing pants trimmed with small metal discs that jingled as they moved out of my way.

"Sorry," I said, not losing pace.

We stopped near the tuxedos and huddled. Sam said, "Okay, Caroline go to Toys. J.J., you go to Linens."

Linens? I wasn't going to be able to search for a new look in Linens.

"J.J.?" Caroline asked, forgetting, or not noticing, that I'd changed my name earlier.

"That's what my friends call me." I waited a beat for her approval. I didn't get it. It felt like a sting.

Caroline left without much of a run.

Sam said, "I'm going to Garden." He went to the escalator.

"Wait," I called. "Which way to Linens?"

He pointed to the "lift" and held up six fingers.

"And what do I do when I get there?"

"You text a clue about where you are, like, 'Cover me up, I'm cold.'" And Sam disappeared up the escalators.

"Wait!"

He started walking down the upward-moving stairs. "What?"

"I don't have anyone's cell phone numbers."

He ran down faster and jumped the last few steps to return to the landing. "Gimme your digits. I'll text everyone. Then you'll have 'em all."

I told him my number, and he practically shoved me into the elevator.

Downstairs I found Linens and looked for a place to hide. There were thousands of possibilities. Behind a pile of towels, under a display bed that was wrapped in pretty sheets and comforters, among stacks of blankets . . . But a fake tub caught my eye, mostly because I thought of a great clue: "Rub-a-dub-dub."

I opened my phone and saw a text from Sam. I guess he'd already found a hiding spot, because he'd sent everyone a note that said, "Rhymes with noses." Since he was in Garden, I guessed he was hidden among roses, although it could've been hoses.

I replied to everyone with my awesome clue and pulled back the display shower curtain that partially hid a claw-foot bathtub. When it seemed like no one was looking, I casually pulled the curtain aside and slipped behind it.

The tub was filled with light pink plastic balls that looked like bubbles. I dug a foot in between the balls, and when I touched the bottom of the tub, I put the other foot in too. I carefully sunk into the bubbles until I was completely covered. I only left myself a little crack to watch the back side of the shower curtain so I'd know when someone pushed it aside.

The tub was surprisingly comfortable. Cozy, actually. I wanted to shop rather than play this game, which wasn't as dumb as I thought it would be, but now that I was lying here, it felt good.

I yawned and waited.

8

No one came.

After a long time—I'm not sure how long because I fell asleep—I woke up. I could tell something was different.

Strange.

Dark.

Quiet.

Even a little eerie.

I crept out of my hiding place. The lights in the store were off. There were some dim security lights. I heard a strange slapping sound on the outside wall that was closest to me. It took a minute to get the sleepy fuzz from my eyes and focus on a window. When I did, I saw lots of rain and a flag hanging off the side of the building, flapping viciously in the wind.

What is going on?

I took my phone out of my back pocket and checked it. It was completely blank. *Broken?* I fiddled with the buttons, and the screen lit up. *My butt turned it off!* I dialed the last number that had texted me.

Sam answered, "Where are you?"

"Linens."

"Seriously?"

"Yeah. That's where you told me to go."

Sam said, "Like three hours ago."

Three *hours*? I'd slept in a department store bathtub for three stinkin' hours?

"Where are *you*? Did you get found?" I peeked around a display of purple towels in search of another human. No one was in the dark room. A chill went up the entire back of my boring body, telling me this was anything but dull; it was bad.

"Found? No. J.J., are you off your trolley? The game is over. It's been over. The store lost electricity in this storm. Everyone had to leave. Where have you been?"

What storm? I had a dreadful feeling that I'd just woken up in the middle of a scene from a horror movie, and I was the main character. We had crossed exciting and gone to scary. I wondered if I'd rather be bored. "So no fish and chips?" I asked. I couldn't think of anything else to say, and besides worrying about being slashed by a department store killer, I had food on the brain, in a big way.

"We *had* chips a while ago without you," Sam said. "We thought maybe you found the Dress-Up Department or you got to demo an electric car or something better than dinner." Well, dang. Now I was hungry, scared, sans a new outfit, and *also* bummed I didn't demo an electric car. "We stayed in the store as long as we could looking for you. You didn't answer your phone. What's 'Rub-a-dub-dub'?"

"You know the poem 'Rub-a-dub-dub, three men in a tub'?"

There was an odd pause. "None of us knew what that clue meant."

"What floor are you on?" I asked. "I'll come find you."

"No floor," Sam said. "I'm across the street. The store closed. As in the doors are locked."

My mouth went dry. "What are you saying?"

"I'm trying to say that you're locked in."

If this was a horror movie, really spooky music would've played right at that moment. A lump formed in my throat as I finally grasped the very dire situation.

"I'm all alone."

"Not exactly," Sam said. "There's Ham."

"There's a ham?" A sandwich sounded really good right about now.

"A bloke named Hamlet. He's the night security guard," Sam said.

"I'll find him, and he can let me out."

"No!"

"Why not?"

"DO NOT let Hamlet see you," he said. "He caught Caroline last time we played Slip Away. She got in a heap of trouble. He called her dad, who sent Hamlet a sack of money to let us out of the store's security office. He said he wouldn't do it again; next time he'd ban her from the store."

"Do I really have to stay in here all night?" I asked, panicked.

"That's an option, but we have a plan. We're arranging to rescue you."

"What? How?" Then I heard footsteps coming from Linens. "Someone's coming," I whispered to Sam.

"I know."

"Is it Hamlet? Is he going to take me to security and handcuff me to a chair?"

An arm shoved the shower curtain aside. It was Caroline. She looked royally mad. "There you are."

"Thank God it's you," I said, sitting up. A few plastic bubbles fell out of the tub and rolled across the floor, disappearing underneath a nearby bed.

"You've gotten us into quite a jam."

"I didn't do it on purpose. I fell asleep. You know, jet lag and all."

"What I know is that my friends left the store before it closed, and I stayed in here looking for you, and now we're snookered."

"You got locked in on purpose to look for me?" I guess she had started to like me. She was worried about me.

She continued, "There's no way I could go home to my stepmum without you. If I lost our abroad student, she would make my life miserable. After all, that is her purpose in life."

Or maybe she wasn't concerned about *me* at all.

I followed Caroline to the escalators, which were turned off. We walked down in a crouched position, below the handrail so that we couldn't be seen by anyone (well, Hamlet) who might be on one of the landings.

"Where are you going?" I whispered.

"To the door."

"If the store is closed, don't you think the doors will be locked?"

"Yes, Madam Obvious, I think the doors will be locked." She clucked her tongue like I was a total idiot. She quickly sent a text message. A minute later we were on the ground floor at one of the many sets of big glass doors. We hid behind a tower of boxes wrapped like pretty presents for a party at Buckingham Palace.

Sam appeared on the other side of the glass doors, on the sidewalk in the rain, and started knocking. He looked pretty wet, but it seemed like it had eased up since I'd looked out the window in Linens. When Hamlet didn't come, Sam knocked louder.

I heard a set of feet wearing wet shoes squeak through Purses to the door. Hamlet removed a clunky set of keys from a clip on his belt and turned several locks on the door.

"What is it?" he asked Sam. "Store's closed."

"Thank goodness you're here, sir," Sam said urgently. "I got home from shopping and realized I didn't have my wallet." He made a desperate face. "My mum is gonna kill me. I'm serious. She's loony. If I come home without her credit card, she'll bloody flip." His eyes were surrounded by raindrops that could easily be mistaken for tears.

Hamlet said, "Calm down. She'll understand."

"You don't know her. She's off the north side of the cliffs, if you know what I mean."

Hamlet's eyebrows shot up like he couldn't believe this kid was so afraid of his mother.

"I think I left it at Lively's, which is another problem. If I tell her that, she'll remind me of how fat I am. I'm not supposed to have sweets."

Sam was NOT fat, but the detail added to the picture of his allegedly psycho mother. I had to clap a hand over my mouth to keep myself from giggling.

He continued. "But sometimes I can't help myself. They have the best tarts."

Hamlet patted his chubby stomach. "Don't I know it."

"Can I get it? The wallet, not a tart. I promise, no tarts."

"Sorry, lad. I can't let anyone in after closing. Rules. But wait out here, and I'll take a look at Lively's. If I see it, I'll bring it out, eh?"

Sam shivered more. "Oh, okay, thanks." He gave his teeth a chatter.

Hamlet stood aside. "Come in and stand here and wait. Don't move." He eyed Sam carefully. "I mean it."

Sam stepped inside and stood in front of the unlocked door. As soon as Hamlet was out of sight, we would all dash through the unlocked door.

Hamlet tried to reach around Sam to get to the locks. Sam kept going in the wrong direction and getting in the way. The two of them sidestepped in an awkward dance in which Sam was always in the wrong place.

"Step aside, lad," Hamlet finally said. He released the key ring from his belt, and just as he was about to twist the locks, Ellie came running up to the door.

"Wait," she called, raising her arms like she was protesting.

"We're closed," Hamlet said through the glass door.

"That's my brother." She pointed at Sam. "And . . . and . . . ummm . . . I cannot let you . . . umm . . . You can't kidnap him!" she said, her voice rising about thirteen octaves.

"Kidnap?"

"Yes, that's what I said. Kidnap. Now let him go or I'll call the police right now." She held up her phone.

Ham pushed the door open. "No one's kidnapping anyone."

She made an act of calming herself down. "Oh, okay, then. As long as that's settled." She looked at him and searched for something else to say. "Nice keys. Do you lock all the doors?"

She was being so totally obvious.

"Yeah. That's my job. Now you and your brother, neither of which I am kidnapping, clear off. I'll check for your wallet, but only if you get out right now. Otherwise you'll have to come back tomorrow."

They stepped outside. Ellie casually left her toe in the door, keeping it open just a smidge. Did she really think that was going to work?

Hamlet released the bulky key ring for a third time and reached for the highest lock. He immediately saw the crack in the door. Looking down, he noticed Ellie's foot. "Do you mind?"

She pulled it out. "Not at all," she said.

Hamlet twisted the locks and walked away, turning occasionally to watch them argue on the sidewalk.

Not surprisingly, a few minutes later Hamlet returned empty-handed, and with a slight hint of powdered sugar around his mouth. I turned off the flash and took a picture of the man. I figured that if I was going to photo-document this trip, I might as well start with Hamlet.

Without unlocking the glass doors, he yelled, "No wallet!" He turned away, and his squeaky shoes took him back toward the Hall of Gourmets. My stomach sank.

Sam and Ellie walked away, heads down. Drenched.

Caroline's phone vibrated. She showed me a text from Sam. "Fail. You're stuck."

Caroline didn't send a reply.

"What are we gonna do?" I asked. If my mom found out that I was locked in a department store on my first night in London, she'd make me come home right away. My whole trip would be blown.

She exhaled. "There's only one thing we can do."

"Turn ourselves in to Hamlet?"

"Um, no. Think again."

No escape? No turn-in?

She tapped a few texts. Then she snapped her phone shut and put it in her purse. "Stepmum and Dad think we're sleeping at Ellie's. Ellie, Gordo, and Sam know the cover story and they'll meet us in the morning." Caroline headed for the escalator. "If we're locked in here all night, we're going to SHOP!"

9

Finally! I can get my new look after all!

"What about Hamlet?" I asked to the back of her head.

"There are eighteen floors. We'll just have to stay a few behind him as he does his rounds."

"What about the security cameras?" I pointed to one mounted on a wall in a corner.

"J.J., this may be the luckiest day ever, because those cameras are not on. There is usually a little green blinking light. Perhaps when the electricity is out, the cameras go out too."

"I guess that *is* lucky," I said, staring at the camera. She was right; nothing was blinking.

We walked up the escalator and stopped when we heard Hamlet humming "A Spoonful of Sugar" from *Mary Poppins*.

Caroline said, "We canNOT get caught. That would ruin my life. Got it?"

Caroline and I stayed a floor behind Hamlet, so we would know where he was. While he did his security thing on the floor above us, we stopped at Cosmetics and Jewelry.

Just enough light from the moon and a few emergency bulbs allowed us to see. We wandered over to one of the counters, and Caroline found a white smock and a palette of colors. "Might as well give you a makeover."

Maybe Caroline's sixth sense was better than Sam's, because it was like she was reading my mind. Or maybe I really looked like I needed a makeover, which sort of hurt my feelings, even if it was the same thing I'd been thinking all along.

"You could use a bit more color around your eyes," she said, and proceeded to brush powders onto my eyelids. Her art project continued with liner, mascara, fat brushes of bronzer and blush, and finally lipstick.

Before I looked in the mirror, I told myself this was

the first glimpse of the new me. I could wash it off if I hated it. I just really wanted to love it. She spun the stool around. "Voilà," she said.

I opened my eyes. "Wow!"

"I know, eh? There was, like, this totally cute person just waiting to come out."

Well, she didn't say that right, but maybe a compliment was hidden in there. The colors she'd chosen were natural. They brightened everything—my eyes, my skin. It looked really good.

"Wait till we get to the salon and I can do something with your hair."

That definitely didn't sound nice. I'd always liked my hair, but now I thought it could use a refresh to go with this face.

We spritzed the perfume testers as we walked by. We got back on the frozen escalators and walked up until we heard Hamlet humming on the floor above Shoes.

Caroline was drawn to the Shoe Department like a cat to a bowl of warm milk—which reminded me of how hungry I was.

She tried on several shoes that were on display, then approached a door behind the cash register.

With a display boot in her hand, she said, "The stuff in the back is always the be-all. Come on."

I wasn't sure about "be-all," but I think she meant that the shoes in the back were really good.

She turned the doorknob, and we went in. She did something on her phone, and it let out a strong glow. "Flashlight app," she explained. The light revealed towers and towers of shoe boxes. She grinned. "Hello there, my darlings. I'm here, and I'm going to try you all on. All you size thirty-sevens, that is."

Thirty-sevens? Clearly they had different sizing in England than we did.

She showed me how to find the style number on the display shoe and then on the box. The boxes were well organized, so finding what we were looking for was easy.

Moments later I was strolling around in brown flats.

Caroline looked at the shoes I'd chosen. "I'll pick some for you. Do you usually wear jeans like that?"

"Sometimes I wear leggings."

"Of course," she said, like leggings were not the be-all.

I found a mirror and studied my made-up face while I waited. Maybe I'd buy some makeup.

Caroline returned with three boxes. "Try these."

I opened one, then the others. "These are all heels. I wear jeans."

"Who says you can't wear heels with jeans? It's not like they're stilettos."

I hesitated, but I tried on the peepy-toed shoes. (I think that's what they're called.) I walked a bit. They weren't bad. In fact, they were easier to walk in than I thought they'd be. My legs felt longer. I looked in the mirror. Heels looked good with jeans. Who knew?

I guess Caroline did, since I actually liked all three pairs that she had picked out for me.

Caroline tried on really outrageous boots, like with glitter. Somehow they worked for her. After trying a few more on, she came back into the room with a big paper shopping bag. "They look really good. You should take those."

"What? Steal them? No. No way."

"No. Not steal. There's no need to nick. We have an account here. We can just set everything aside and ring it all up in the morning when the store opens."

"Seriously?"

"Quite." We continued to try on shoes—lots of them. I even snapped some pictures so that I'd remember the ones I liked but had left behind. I also shot a short video of our feet in different shoes walking up and down the aisle between the towers of shoes.

We continued to stay far enough from Hamlet as he went about his rounds. We made another stop in Teen Fashions.

Caroline picked out all kinds of clothes for me. I stayed in the dressing room, and she threw stuff over the top.

I paraded around like a runway model, feeling transformed. One shirt didn't have straps (none!), another had swinging fringes, some pants were tight to the ankles, others swayed while I walked. I felt glamorous. Pretty. Totally un-boring.

After an hour of mixing and matching, I decided to wear a new pair of skinny jeans, a long tank top, and a wide belt that rested just below my waist. I added a pair of boots I'd just gotten. They were high—like horseback riding boots. I loved this outfit too much to take it off. Caroline managed to snip the tags and gathered them in a small bag, so that we could pay for it all later and get the security tags removed.

After a little while I'd filled two more shopping bags and taken another video of myself by holding my camera out and trying to capture the outfit.

Finally we were at the salon. Caroline added the flashlight app to my phone, so we had two. I sat in a beautician's chair and spun around in it. She held up a device that looked like a small sandwich maker. "This is a flat iron. It should be your best friend."

She took a section of my hair and put it between two pieces of flat metal, then clamped them shut, sandwiching my hair in between. Then she pulled gently and the iron slid from the crown of my head to the tips of the hair.

"If you do that at home, it will come out pencil straight. Of course, it's not hot now because we don't have electricity." I thought my hair was straight already. She brushed it out and sprayed it with some stuff that made it look supershiny.

Then Caroline took a small piece of my hair and rubbed a stinky-smelling cream on it.

I stiffened. "What is that? Chemicals?" I'd never had any chemicals in my hair. What if she didn't know what she was doing?

"Relax. I've watched my stylist do this a hundred times." She held up a jar of hair lotion that clearly said "blond" on it. "If you don't like it, you can always put the color back in."

"What? You're taking color *out*?" Maybe I wasn't meant to handle un-boring. My heart pounded.

"It's all the rage. Trust me on this. I know what I'm talking about."

A minute later she washed the small section of my hair in the sink and combed it out. I had a streak of blond hair. I couldn't stop staring at it, because I didn't believe it. . . . It looked fantastic, red-carpet fantastic. I *never* felt this glam. And I liked the way it felt. She put in a couple of bobby pins, and the hairstyle looked even better.

On our way out Caroline took a flat iron and added it to my bag. That's when we heard something.

Someone was humming "New York, New York."

We froze.

10

With no time to hide, we clicked off the flashlight apps and stood perfectly still. *Perfectly.*

Hamlet was an older man. He shuffled along without stopping at the salon, steadily proceeding to the next escalator, which he was forced to walk up, since it wasn't moving. Once he was past us, Caroline said, "Do you know what that means?"

"What?"

"He has already checked all the floors above us. We can go all around now and not worry about getting caught."

"Don't you think he'll come back?"

"Why would he? He's done his thing. It's not like people are just going to materialize and gallivant around dressing up and making over."

"It isn't?"

She laughed. "No. Now, let's go to the Dress-Up Department and gallivant."

"Like in dresses?" I asked.

"Not in any ordinary dresses. Wait until you see this."

I followed her up another floor, to Formal Wear. The landing area was set up like a prom with a disco ball, and mannequins in tuxedos and glittery gowns. We ran past the racks of dresses until we got to a back corner that was a medieval castle. It wasn't decorated to look like a palace; it actually *was* a palace built *inside* the store. Mannequins of knights stood guard.

Caroline walked over a bridge and into the palace. It was packed with trunks of crowns, necklaces, scarves, and scepters. Shelves of Styrofoam heads wore wigs: straight red hair, blond braids, jet-black pixie cut.

Along the walls were hanging displays of every kind of gown you could imagine. Some were bustled and bunched up at the back, while others had long trains draped behind them. There were also costumes for boys and men: a British policeman uniform; a yeoman uniform, which was a one-piece black kilt with red trim and an embroidered red crown on the chest; and a royal guard with a red jacket, black pants, and a hat that looked like a giant black Q-tip.

This palace was like the biggest box of dress-up clothes imaginable.

I chose a wig that was a half mile high in tight brown curls, and a velvet gown suitable for a coronation, then disappeared behind a pretty white screen with little pink flowers painted all over it.

Caroline grabbed a tight, red satin dress with spaghetti straps and a hot pink wig. She played music on her mobile and we changed, and then we danced around in our fancy outfits.

I put my phone on a ledge and set it to video-record us dancing around. But the ledge was low, so I probably cut our heads off. I didn't care. It wasn't like this would go into the montage. I was having the best time of my life and I wanted it photo-documented. "I love this place," I said.

"If you think this rocks, I can show you something even more fab."

"No way. Better than this?"

"Follow me." She went toward the Hole and paused. "Shh."

I stood silently.

She listened. "No humming. No squeaky shoes. The coast is clear. Let's move on." She ran up the escalator.

I tugged up my dress and followed her toward the Children's Department. I couldn't imagine what we were going to do there until I saw it: a trampoline the size of my backyard. It was surrounded by an enchanted garden.

Caroline kicked off her shoes, climbed on, and started bouncing. I joined her, jumping higher and higher. Finally I held my breath and gathered the layers of my gown in one hand and flipped backward, landing triumphantly on my feet.

"Wow! How did you learn to do that?" she asked.

"Gym class, I guess." I plopped on my butt and popped up. "Try that."

She did, and she giggled the whole time.

I tried to get some real action videos with my phone, but with all the bouncing and wig hair, I'm not sure what I got.

I bounced myself sweaty and eventually flopped onto the springy floor, flat on my back as I tried to catch my breath.

"Something wrong?" Caroline asked.

"I'm pooped."

"I'm a bit zonked myself," she said. "I know where we can crash for the night . . . like real princesses."

"Really?"

"The Furniture Department is just one floor up."

"And they have beds?"

"Big, beautiful beds."

"I'm there," I said.

A few minutes later we were back in our regular clothes and tucked into side-by-side king beds. We chose two that couldn't be seen with a quick glance from the hallway. And for a little extra insurance, we took a wooden screen like would be used to separate a room into two parts and relocated it to shield the beds.

I sank my head onto a feather pillow and almost fell asleep instantly, thinking about my first day in London. I had set out for an experience to change my life, but got so much more. I was changing my life *and* my image. This trip *had* become an adventure. It had been a wonderful day, trapped-in-a-mega-department-store-slash-carnival wonderful.

Caroline had started out not liking me, but now I thought she was my friend. "I had a great time today," I said. "Thanks."

She said nothing.

I turned to look at her. Her eyes were closed and she was breathing deeply.

I started falling into a dream about *The Wizard of Oz*, when I realized I wasn't dreaming. Someone was humming "Over the Rainbow."

11

I peeked under the oriental screen and saw Hamlet's wet shoes making their way over to us. Apparently he didn't go to sleep. He *did* go through his rounds a second time.

I grabbed a few big pillows and covered Caroline with them as my heart climbed into my throat. I did a good job, because I couldn't even tell she was in the bed.

His steps got closer, and my panic rose higher in my stomach. I pulled the comforter back up so my bed would look made, and then I got down on my belly and crawled under it.

Hamlet came right up to the screen and switched songs to "Tomorrow" from *Annie*. I held my breath and prayed Caroline wouldn't move or snore. I could see the thick soles of his squeaky orthopedic shoes come behind the wooden screen. A few more steps, and I could reach out and touch his toes.

Then he turned and left.

By the time he was at "I just stick out my chin and grin and say . . . ," it sounded like he was back at the Hole.

I got back into bed and fell asleep.

Quickly.

Deeply.

It seemed like I was only out for a few seconds when Caroline woke me, but according to my watch it was eight a.m. "You sleep like the dead. I thought I'd never be able to knock you awake," she said. "Let's get out of here."

I put my shoes on, made the bed, and got my backpack. We walked down the frozen escalator all the way to the Purse Department. "You going to pick one out?" Caroline asked.

I thought my pack worked just fine for me. "Sure. I mean, you're sure we're going to pay for it?"

"I promise we'll pay for it. I don't know if I can say the same for breakfast, though."

"What breakfast?"

"The one we're going to take from Lively's. And, J.J., I do mean 'take,' like steal. Sebastian can't spit on it if he's not there, and technically you paid for tarts yesterday that were rubbish; so he owes you."

When she put it that way, I didn't feel bad about taking tarts from Sebastian. However, even though Caroline and I had an awesome night, I believed she'd probably been very mean to Sebastian and deserved to be cut off from his tarts.

I picked out a purse using a very scientific method I like to call eenie-meenie-miney-mo. Caroline nodded her approval, so I guess I'd eenie-meenie-ed a good brand and style.

From behind the counter at Lively's, we slid the pastry case open. Caroline took a scone and bit into it with an "Mmmm."

I took one too. I had to agree. It was like dessert-for-breakfast good. Caroline threw a big white box at me. "Fill that."

"Really?"

"For as long as he's been withholding these awesome treats from us, yes. Fill it."

I took my backpack off so that I could reach inside the case. I chose a mix of different pastries so that it wouldn't be obvious that we'd ransacked the shelves.

Caroline took out my phone and made a video of me half inside the case. She narrated a pretend documentary, "Desperate for carbs after a long night of mischief while locked inside Daphne's, the creature snatches countless pastries—"

An overhead light came on and surprised her.

"Ohmigod the power's back on. Get your bum out of there," she whispered. "We gotta hide from the security cameras."

I removed myself from the case and followed Caroline to a hiding place that was *not* in front of a mirror but behind a stone statue of a naked man with leaves covering the . . . essentials.

It was a half hour until opening, and the store workers filed in to prepare the Hall of Gourmets for the day.

I thought for sure a worker would spot us and know we'd been there all night, but nobody came to our little corner behind the naked statue. We hung out for another twenty or thirty minutes after the store finally opened and customers entered. Then, very calmly, as if we'd just done some early-morning shopping, Caroline casually walked to a register and paid for the items we'd accumulated throughout the night.

Sam, Ellie, and Gordo were waiting for us on the sidewalk.

"You survived?" Ellie asked. "How was it? What did you do? Ohmigosh. I have majorly good news—I found my turtle earring that I thought I'd lost." She pointed to her ear. "I was getting out of the shower and—POW!—I saw it on the floor in the corner. I mean, what are the odds of that? And—"

Caroline cut her off. "It was a nightmare being locked in the nirvana of shopping all night, but we survived."

Gordo said, "Now, *that's* good news."

Ellie said, "J.J., I love your hair like that."

My cheeks warmed. "Thanks," I said, shrugging like it was no big deal. At least it was dry now. And I could try out that flat iron when we got back to Caroline's house. In fact, I was psyched to try it. "We had a ton of time to kill."

I caught Sam staring at me. Self-consciously my hands went to my newly-dyed hair. "Something wrong?"

"No," he said. "Um, how did you make out? You . . . look . . . look different."

"*Good* different?"

"Um, there was nothing wrong before, but yeah,

good." This time he turned his head, allowing longish hairs to cover his face.

My insides jumped up and yelled, *Yay!* I had no idea what it would feel like to get a compliment like that from a boy. A cute British boy. And it felt—well, it "took the biscuit." They say that, right?

I said to Sam, "You look good too." He did in an untucked, crisply ironed oxford.

I held up the Lively's box. "I got something for you. No spit."

"Aces!" He took the box and popped a lemon square into his mouth.

I asked him, "What is that sound? Is that the Hungry Club calling?"

Sam laughed at my impersonation of him.

Ellie and Caroline slowly inched themselves away from us and talked in whispers. I was a little bummed that I wasn't included in their secret chat.

I figured since I had just had an incredible night with Caroline, we were friends, right? And rather than standing with the boys, I could move over to the girls' area and see what was going on, right?

I could be like: "Hey, guys, latte?"

Or maybe: "What's up, girlfriends?"

Perhaps: "That was so awesome, eh?"

I decided I'd go with: "It's gonna be hard to find something to top that today, huh?"

I took a step closer to the whispers and was ready to give my line, when I heard Caroline saying, "It was soooo boring . . ." Quickly I turned before they could tell that I'd heard.

She didn't have a fun time last night? There's no way she was that good an actress. She must have been talking about something else. I pretended to look through my Daphne's bag and listened hard to see if I could get anything else.

Ellie said, "She's from a small town in America. Things are different there."

"Yeah. Lame," Caroline said. "It was like she'd never been in a store before."

"But isn't that exciting for *you*? You can, like, teach her. You know, like in that vampire movie. When Priscilla, the two-hundred-year-old vampiress, had to show the new vamp how to hunt."

"Oh, I love that picture," Caroline said. "But she's not a newborn vampire."

Sam called over to me, interrupting me from eavesdropping on the rest of the conversation. "Hey!" He was holding up his cell phone. "It says it's you calling." I wasn't making a call. "Are you dialing me with your bum?" he joked.

Instantly my hands went to the back pocket of my new skinny jeans. No phone.

He picked it up and listened. His expression changed from amused to annoyed. "Hello, Sebastian."

Sebastian? From my phone? Where is my phone?

I looked around.

My backpack—it wasn't here.

I had left it in the store.

At Lively's.

My stomach plunged to my knees. I'd left my backpack at the scene of the crime!

Sam's expression flattened. "He's sending us a list." Touching the screen of his mobile, he saw it and read it out loud for us. "It says: salon, trampoline, unmade beds, costumes, shoe department, and stolen electronics . . ." Sam looked at me and Caroline. "What's he talking about?"

Gordo asked, "What the heck did you guys do? And why did you steal stuff?"

Caroline assured him, "We didn't steal anything."

Sam added, "And there were items taken from the bakery."

"Except a few items from the bakery," Caroline said. Gordo gave her a questioning look. "Seriously."

Gordo said, "He must think it was you guys."

Ellie added, "Tell the midget to prove it!"

"How does he have your phone?" Caroline asked me with an angry tone.

"I must've left my backpack behind his counter."

"That's just bril, J.J.," Caroline snapped, and it hurt. All the wonderfulness of the most exciting night I ever had in my life melted into a bazillion pieces like it never happened.

Ellie said, "That doesn't prove anything. You could've left your backpack there yesterday. Someone saw it lying around and tossed it behind Lively's counter like it was a sack of tomatoes." She said it like *to-mah-toes*. "And no one saw it until the morning."

Gordo corrected her, "Potatoes." *Po-tah-toes*.

"Exactly," Ellie agreed.

"Simply genius," Caroline said to me, not listening to the possible *po-tah-to* explanation, which I thought was good.

Well, she may be mad at me, but this definitely isn't boring.

Ellie looked at Sam's phone some more. "I'm loving that wig."

12

"Wig?" Caroline barked. She snatched the cell phone out of Sam's hands. "Oh, how great is this? He has the photos and videos. He can prove we were in the store last night."

Sam spoke to Sebastian on the cell phone, not his finger-phone. "I'll come in now and get the backpack and the mobile. And I'll pay you for the sweets. You should take it as a compliment; we love them."

Under her breath Caroline said, "It's *you* we hate."

Sam seemed to be listening to Sebastian. "Hang on. Calm down. I'm gonna put you on the speaker so everyone can hear your ranting." He pushed the button and held the cell phone out for us to hear.

Sebastian was already talking. "—don't bother coming in to pick it up, because I'm not giving it back."

Gordo said, "Don't get your knickers in a twist, Sebastian boy. We can work something out."

"Yes, we can, Gordo. I already have."

"What do you mean?" Sam asked.

"Here's the deal," Sebastian said. "I have a paper due in four days. It's about the demotion of our poor planet Pluto. You guys are going to write it for me. I will get two hundred and fifty words of this paper e-mailed to me at eight o'clock every night for three nights. Then, on Friday morning I'll e-mail it to my teacher. If I don't get them—"

"If you don't get them, then what?" Gordo tested him.

"I'll tell you!" Sebastian snapped. He paused, drawing out the suspense. "I'll tell everyone that you guys committed the crime in the store last night! And then, oh my, I wonder what they'll do? Maybe arrest you? Maybe ban you from the store?"

Caroline looked shocked, even horrified by these threats. Her eyes narrowed and her mouth crinkled with anger.

Ellie smacked her hand over her mouth to cover her own shock. Then she shot out questions: "Really? Would they seriously do that? What exactly would that mean? Like banned from the store *forever*?"

Gordo took Ellie's hands in his and lifted them up to her mouth. Quietly he said, "Shh. Please?" That seemed to work well, because she pressed her lips tightly together and nodded.

"Okay. Fine," Sam said. "Continue with your threat, which doesn't really make any sense, because nothing was stolen except a few tarts, which I offered to pay for."

Sebastian continued, "From the photographic proof in my hand, it looks like two of your merry band were in this store after closing, making a terrible mess, and I can only conclude that if they were here when the electronics were stolen, then they were involved. I'm quite sure the police will see it that way."

"But we didn't steal anything," Caroline chimed in.

"So, it's purely coincidental that you were in the store on the same night there was a major theft. Maybe you believe that, but I'm not so sure that the authorities would understand. I find it hard to believe myself," he said. "Look, as long as I get my two hundred and fifty words each night, you have nothing to worry about. And they'd better be good. No plagiarism."

Ellie yelled to the phone, "You're a cheater!" Gordo touched a finger to her lip, and that reminded her she was supposed to be quiet.

Caroline asked, "So all we have to do is write your blooming paper and we can forget about all of this?"

"Well, there's one more teeny tiny little detail."

Sam growled, "What?"

"I need at least a B-plus, and no one—I repeat, NO ONE—can know that I didn't write it. This paper is vitally important to my future. Do you *capisce* what I'm saying to you? Very important."

We grumbled our understanding into the phone. "Yeah, yeah, we *capisce*," Ellie said.

"I've copied the videos and photos onto a flash drive. By the way, how stupid can you be to create evidence like this?" he asked, not waiting for an answer. "The paper is due via e-mail at ten Friday morning. And because it is critical, the teacher is going to be checking references and grading pretty quickly."

"Why is she grading it so fast?" Sam asked.

"Did you miss the part when I said 'vitally important'?" Sebastian barked. "Once I get my grade, we'll meet and I'll give you the flash drive. For now Ellie can come in and get this phone. No one else. I can't stand to see your ugly gobs." He continued, "If you are even one millisecond later than eight o'clock each night, I'll make you an instant Internet video sensation." He laughed evilly.

He had us. He totally had us in a you-are-my-puppet sort of way. We had to do this for him or we'd possibly get arrested.

This was definitely not boring, but ending up in a British prison was not the kind of life-changing experience I was looking for on this trip. I could look forward to being locked in my room, with the exception of school or weeding, for the rest of my life. Suddenly I was keenly interested in Pluto.

"Why can't you do the paper yourself?" Sam asked.

"That's none of your beeswax either. Just do it. Fast."

"He's bluffing," Gordo said to Sam, loud enough for Sebastian to hear.

The phone made a jerking sound on the other end. Sebastian said, "Oh my goodness gracious, what just happened? What did I do? Did I just accidentally upload one of those incriminating videos? I think I did." He ended the call.

Caroline hissed, "He didn't."

Sam showed us his screen. It was a video of me and Caroline—well, our feet—trying on shoes. Lots of shoes. The clip didn't show our faces.

"Un-bloody-believable," Caroline said. "Let's do this ridiculous Pluto paper for that pastry midget. We can work at my house."

Things were getting more un-boring by the minute. Maybe a little too de-bored-ified.

"First I'm getting that phone," Sam said. He stormed into Daphne's and came back a few seconds later with a flush to his cheeks and no phone in his hands.

Gordo patted Ellie's back. "Can you handle it?"

Ellie made a muscle with her arms. "See these guns?" She walked into the store. A minute later she returned with a mini multicolored layered cake.

"What is that?" I asked.

"A petit four. Isn't it cute? It's like a little rainbow baby sandwich made of cake. Wanna bite?"

"No, thanks," I said, but I was still hungry. I had heard about this thing called a full English breakfast. Supposedly everyone ate it. Where was it now? None of my new friends knew how popular it was, obviously.

"No luck with the phone?" Gordo asked.

"Oh, that." She popped the remaining little morsel of petit four into her mouth and reached into her back pocket. "Here you go."

"How'd you do that?" Gordo asked.

"I have my ways," Ellie said. "But don't get too excited.

He showed me the flash drive, a little plastic worm. It's very adorable, actually. And fitting, because he's like a worm." She handed me my new phone with the hi-res camera, and I thought that maybe the decision to do a photo montage of my trip wasn't such a good idea after all.

13

Sam asked, "Don't you think he's made other copies of the videos and photos?"

"We'll have to worry about copies later," Gordo said. "But I think we shouldn't trust anything Sebastian says."

We crammed into a taxi, which made me feel like I was a gum ball inside a machine. It took us to the Metro station. "It's a fifteen-minute train ride to Brentwood," Sam explained.

We sat on the train, and I couldn't help thinking for a second about the Hogwarts Express. Of course, this was nothing like Harry Potter's train. It was shiny and modern, with half of the seats facing one way and the other half facing the other way.

"Shh," Sam said. "Look at the telly." He indicated a flat screen in the front of the train car. Two news reporters stood in front of Daphne's.

The female reporter said, *"Shortly after opening this morning, Daphne's employees discovered that several thousand pounds' worth of electronic equipment was missing. The investigation is just beginning and we'll certainly report details on this case as they unfold."* The name "Skye Summers" was written on the screen under her face.

The male reporter, Cole Miles, said, *"Indeed, Skye, what does surveillance footage from the Daphne's security system show?"*

"It seems that with the big power outage last night, the whole system was down. Authorities are presently looking for the night watchman for answers," Skye said.

Cole said, *"More on the Daphne's theft later. But now to sports. Let's talk about football."* The screen switched to a scene of what I would call a soccer game.

"There really was a theft last night," Caroline said. "What are the chances of that?"

"You tell us," Ellie said.

"What do you mean?" Caroline asked.

"I mean, why would you take that stuff? It's not like you need it."

Caroline snapped at her, "We didn't steal anything. Do you see any stolen electronics?"

"No," Ellie said sheepishly.

"Exactly." Then under her breath I think she said, "Idiot." *What kind of person calls her friend an idiot?*

Gordo said, "The police will figure this all out. Don't worry your pretty little fashionable heads about it."

I forced a smile. I hoped Gordo was right, because the videos and photos that Sebastian had would surely put Caroline and me at the scene of the crime *during the crime.*

From the train station we walked a few blocks to meet Liam, who was supposedly picking us up after we'd all met for breakfast following the sleepover at Ellie's. On the ride I clicked an e-mail to my mom and dad. My mom had probably scrubbed every surface of the house worrying about me.

Approaching the manor house, I was again reminded of how big and fabulous it was. Ivy and moss crept everywhere.

We planted ourselves in her kitchen while Caroline got her iPad. "I cannot believe Sebastian has the nerve to blackmail me. He is more of a weasel than I thought. Just thinking about him makes me feel all icky." She rubbed her arms.

Liam brought us an assortment of juices and baby-size muffins. *Yay, Liam!* I was starving, so I popped one into my mouth whole. I saw Sam look at me, and I thought he was going to call the Hungry Police, but he didn't. The next muffin I took, I broke and ate in smaller pieces.

Mrs. Littleton stepped into the kitchen. "Oh, hi there, gang. Jordan, I got an early text from your mama. She was a wee bit angry when she got your message that said all y'all have done is shop and have a pillow party."

"Pillow party?" Caroline asked, confused.

"You call it a sleepover, but we used to call that a pillow party in my sorority days," Mrs. Littleton said.

I thought for sure that Ellie was going to blow our cover story. She fiddled with the lace table runner. "The pillow party was very . . . pillowy. We had a pillow fight and a pillow pile and um . . . ah . . . uh . . . We made a fortress out of blankets and pillows."

I was officially impressed. I doubted that Ellie with a *y* would have thought so fast on her feet. The fortress was an especially good detail.

"Really? A fort?" Mrs. Littleton asked.

"Yup," Ellie said. "That was J.J.'s idea. Apparently

Americans like to build stuff with blankets and pillows."

"J.J.'s?" Mrs. Littleton looked at me to make sure I was J.J. I nodded. "Cute," she said.

Caroline said, "This was after we spent a positively perfect day at Daphne's."

Mrs. Littleton said, "Did you hear the news that there was a break-in last night? The telly said there had been some mischief and a theft—jewelry, I think."

"Electronics," Ellie corrected her.

Caroline said, "J.J. got some nice additions to her wardrobe. I mean, look at her. Better, eh?"

"I did think there was something different about ya. I thought it was just the blond streak in your hair. Do you think your mama is going to be okay with that?"

"Oh, yes," I lied. "She is totally into exploring new fashion." I really hated lying. "I don't know when you saw her last, but she has become quite a collector of shoes, like Jimmy Choos. Ha! That rhymes." (Last night I'd learned that Jimmy Choos were a really hot brand.)

"A bore," Ellie said.

"What?" I asked. "What did you say?"

"We call someone who collects lots of shoes a *shoe bore*."

"Okay. Right. Well, that's what she is," I lied again. "A bore from a shoe store. Ha!" I did it again.

Mrs. Littleton said, "Well, it sounds like y'all have had great fun. But your mama was peeved that you were shopping instead of working on your school assignment."

Caroline mumbled something like, "Heaven forbid we take a break from studies over school vacation."

"She was?" I asked.

"I haven't heard her so mad since we got splashed with a hose at the homecoming football game. Ohhh, we had been having such a good time until that happened."

"My mom had fun?"

"Oh, all the time! She loved it!"

I was sure she had my mom confused with someone else from college.

Mrs. Littleton said, "But don't worry. I took care of everything. I promised her that you would spend the rest of the week hitting all the places on your list. To calm her down I told her y'all would text pics to her from each sight."

"You can't be serious?" Caroline asked, as though the idea of checking if she was lying was completely absurd, even though she had *just* told a whole story about a sleepover party that never happened. "She wants to spy on us? Why doesn't she just send a babysitter to trail around after us?"

I was totally embarrassed. Even though I was on the other side of the world, my parents were still looking over my shoulder.

"If that's an invitation," Mrs. Littleton said, "I'd love to go with y'all."

"Yay!" Ellie said. "You'll be like one of the gang, except older and more . . . more older than we are."

Caroline pursed her lips in anger, but spoke in a careful and controlled voice, "Um, I think NOT."

Mrs. Littleton said, "Caroline darlin', I gotcha a little something. Come on into your daddy's office so I can give it to you."

"What is it?" Caroline asked.

"Ooh, it's a surprise."

Caroline followed her stepmother out of the room.

"What do you think it is?" Ellie asked.

Gordo shrugged. "Could be anything. Remember the time she got a Vespa scooter? Her mum didn't even know she was too young to drive it."

They returned very quickly. Caroline was smiling.

"What was it?" Sam asked.

"What?" she asked.

"The surprise."

"Oh, it was kinda like a secret surprise. No biggie, really," Caroline said.

"No biggie," Mrs. Littleton confirmed. "So, lemme just get my coat and I'll come along with y'all today."

Caroline said, "As much fun as that would be, I think it's a richer adventure for J.J. to experience London with us, just us, friends her own age." She put her arm over my shoulder and said to me, "You are going to have an awesome time."

"Well, I want J.J. to have the fullest experience possible," Mrs. Littleton said, like it was a big sacrifice for her not to hang out with us.

"That's what we all want," Caroline said. "We'll certainly text you pictures from each sight we visit. Oh, and those pics will be perfect to use for your photo montage assignment." I thought Caroline had quickly changed her mind about sightseeing.

"It'll be heaps of fun, I'm sure," Mrs. Littleton said, and exited the kitchen.

There was a moment of silence. "I think that went well," Ellie said. "She bought the whole fortress thing."

Caroline announced, "I'm going to take a shower. Can you start on planet Pluto? We have to do a super-good job on it so that those videos stay under wraps. If we get discovered, it would be very bad for me."

Gordo said, "Daphne's couldn't ban you for long. You're their best customer."

"Well, I don't want to risk it. Besides, I have more to lose than shopping."

"Like what?" I asked.

"A lot," she said, offering a nonanswer.

As if commanded by the queen bee, Gordo took the seat at the iPad and began telling us what he was writing: "I am Sebastian Lively, and I am a jerk. I am not the one writing this paper because I'm a cheater . . ."

"Stop that," Caroline said. "Don't joke around."

"You're smart," Ellie said to Gordo. "Can't you just whip it out or something?"

"Of course he can," Sam said.

"Bril," Caroline said, and left for her shower.

"Sure," Gordo joked. "I'll write a research paper in the next few minutes while you pals just hang out."

"That works for me," Ellie said. She didn't get that Gordo had been kidding. At least, I'm pretty sure he was.

Gordo googled some sites and sent pages to the printer at the other side of the kitchen. Sam read them over and tossed out random Pluto facts that made me think maybe this could be a good paper.

When Caroline returned to the kitchen, she was surrounded by shower scents. Her wet hair was combed out and hung lower than it had last night. She wore new clothes: a flowy peasant blouse, black jeans, and ankle boots with a heel. I noticed that she had also put on a new palette of makeup. "J.J., Liam left you fresh towels."

As much as I was enjoying working on the paper with Sam and Gordo (Ellie really wasn't into it), I left. I was excited to use my new hair straightener, and makeup, and to wear another new outfit. As I walked down the hall to the bathroom, I heard Sam and Gordo talking about the solar system, and the printer hummed.

I also heard Caroline say to Ellie, "Look, we need to make sure J.J. has a good time, and we have to keep the Bakery Bozo off our backs."

Ellie said, "Where I am, fun follows, and the boys have Pluto under control. No worries, Carrie."

"Don't call me Carrie," Caroline said.

"Gotcha," Ellie said.

I was so happy to hear that Caroline wanted me to have a memorable visit to London. She was sincere, wasn't she?

14

I felt like a celebrity in my new duds, makeup, and straightened hair. I found Ellie thumbing through a fashion magazine while Sam and Gordo huddled over the iPad. When she saw me, Caroline checked me out from hair to shoes. A quick jump of her eyebrows told me she was pleasantly surprised with my look. She dropped her feet from the kitchen table to the floor and said, "She's back. The American of the week." To her friends she said, "We're off to see the sights of London!" Her words sounded excited, but something about her tone said otherwise, I think.

"Oh, yeah," Ellie said. She put on a crocheted wool cap. It was so cute. I never thought of wearing a cap like that. It covered her spiky hair but let her double earrings show. I wanted double earrings and a cap. Maybe I could get those today.

Sam finally stopped reading and caught a glimpse of me. He didn't look long, but brushed some longish hairs in front of his face and packed the iPad in a pack with one strap that he hung diagonally across his chest.

Thankfully, I had my new purse, or I might have been jealous of that pack. I really preferred having free arms, but I liked having a stylish purse too. I flipped my fab hair over the strap. It felt good.

Gordo said "Ooh lala" about my appearance. "Sit tight. I need a minute to freshen up if I'm gonna hang with this one." And then he locked himself in the powder room.

When he returned, his collar was snapped up and I smelled a hint of cologne. We were ready for Liam to take us to the train station.

"Where are we going first?" Gordo asked, looking at his reflection in the steel refrigerator and moving a hair to where he wanted it to be.

"I suppose we should ask J.J.," Caroline said. "This week is all about her."

Normally that would've made me do a *Yay, me!* But something in her voice sounded just a little sarcastic. No one else seemed to notice, so maybe I was being overly sensitive. So: *Yay, me!*

"I'd like to go to the Tower of London," I said, with very little confidence that was the right answer. "I've been dying to go there." Then I laughed because I said "dying." "Get it? Because King Henry killed so many of his wives there?"

Gordo and Sam cracked a bit of a smile at my joke. I didn't think Ellie got it, but she laughed anyway, probably to be polite.

"Then off we go to the Tower," Caroline said. "If we make it quick, we'll have time to see the new zombie picture."

"Oh, right!" Ellie said. "I absolutely cannot wait to see that picture. I hear it's scary and gory. 'The bloodier the better,' that's what I always say." She got her face very close to mine, looked me in the eye, and said, "OOOOH! I am so excited. After the picture maybe we can get manis. I really need one. Look." She held out her hand with chipped black polish.

"Ditto," Gordo said. He held out his hand too, but he didn't have chipped polish. "My cuticles are so bad."

"TD," Ellie said about his nails. No one knew what

she meant. "Total Disaster," she explained to our questioning faces. "Duh."

"Not me," Sam said. His nails were bitten as low as they could go.

"That's fine," Caroline said. "You can work on the Pluto project while we're mani-ing. We've totally got to stay on top of that. I swear if I get in trouble because of that rat, I can't be responsible for what I'll do to him."

Sam didn't seem bothered by being told he'd be working on a research paper. He said, "This assignment isn't hard. I don't know why he can't do it."

"Fab," Caroline said. "Then everything is peachy. We'll jet through the Tower, catch the zombie picture, and get manis."

"Sure," I said, but honestly, I didn't like the idea of rushing through the Tower of London to see a movie I could see at home, or rent on DVD. But getting my nails done sounded like a treat.

As we walked to the car, Caroline added, "I would love to think of a way to get even with the Swine of Sweets for making us do his work for him."

No one commented that Caroline had said "us" even though she wasn't doing anything for the Pluto project. I wondered about a way we could get our videos back and also make sure Sebastian got caught for cheating.

Caroline would probably be psyched if I came up with a plan.

Liam dropped us at the train station, and I followed the gang to the right platform.

Suddenly Gordo stopped and pointed to a screen overhead. "Look at the telly," he said.

The reporter named Skye said, *"As we reported earlier today, there was a break-in at Daphne's, during which some sophisticated electronic equipment was stolen. After a thorough inventory, it was determined that the loss was greater than originally suspected. A selection of power tools was also taken. The combination of items leads authorities to believe the robbers may have been collecting tools necessary for other crimes."*

"What exactly are the items that were stolen?" Cole asked.

"That information hasn't been released, Cole. But an interesting video has been attracting a lot of attention on the Internet. Let's go to the clip."

They ran the video that Sebastian had uploaded of Caroline and me trying on shoes.

"You can see by the date and time stamp that this video was taken at Daphne's. No faces are visible in this clip, but the audio suggests it's a local and an American girl."

Cole asked, *"Are you saying these are the robbers?"*

"Authorities haven't said that, but these girls were in the store after closing on the same night," Skye said. *"I know I'd like to be loose in Daphne's after closing, Cole. Can you imagine?"*

"No I can't, but I'd love it too. For now, let's take a look at the weather."

"That blasted Sebastian!" Caroline said. "Look what he's done. He's tied us to this robbery."

"Was it heavy?" Ellie asked Caroline.

"What?"

"All that stuff?" Ellie asked. "Where did you put it?"

"For the love of the queen! We. Didn't. Steal. Anything!" Caroline barked.

Ellie cowered a bit from the volume, then softly asked, "Are you sure?" Then, after seeing Caroline begin to boil red, loudly she said, "Never mind! I didn't just say that. I swear, I didn't. I heard it, so someone said something, but it wasn't me. Maybe it was a ghost."

"Maybe we should go to the police," I suggested, trying to take the heat off Ellie.

"And tell them what, exactly? That we stayed in the store after closing and ran amok in every department all night long on the same night there was a major theft, but we had nothing to do with it? That sounds like it will work," Caroline said. "Truly bril idea, J.J."

"Maybe we should tell your father," Gordo said. "He's involved with Her Majesty's government, isn't he?"

Caroline looked at Gordo like he was stupid, a total moron.

"You know what?" Gordo asked. "Bad idea. Forget I mentioned it," Gordo said.

"Gladly," she said. "Look, no one can think we did this." She asked Sam, "Can we get this Pluto project done early? And get the flash drive back? I don't like the idea of the Dork of Danishes having photographic proof we were in Daphne's that night."

"Early?" Sam asked. "Sebastian was quite specific about the schedule." (He said "schedule" like "sheh-dyul.") "If we stick to his deadlines, we should be fine." He said to Caroline, "You just can't do anything for three days to make him mad."

15

We stood in front of the Tower of London, which was much more than a single tower. There were multiple Gothic castlelike buildings in the complex.

"Let's get a photo," Caroline said. "J.J., you stand right in front here."

Gordo already had his arm around me with a toothy grin exposed. I hadn't noticed before, but braces must not be popular here, because they needed my orthodontist's digits. Except Caroline, of course, who seemed effortlessly perfect.

Ellie crouched down in front of me and stretched her arms wide as if to say, *Ta-da!*

Gordo reached out to a man walking by and said, "Excuse me, mate. Would you mind snapping our photo?"

The man agreed. Gordo had an arm over Caroline's shoulder and the other over mine.

A second later we had a great shot. It was totally going into my photo montage.

"Let me text this to the stepmummy and Mrs. J.J., and we can move on." Caroline fiddled with the phone. "Maybe this is what it's like for a prisoner to have a tracking anklet that follows their every move."

Was she really comparing texting sightseeing pics to our moms to being a prisoner?

Gordo must've been thinking the same thing, because he asked, "A little dramatic, eh?"

Maybe Caroline liked dramatic. I could do that. "I know, right? It's like going around with a big green ogre on your back."

Ellie jumped in at the mention of an ogre. "Maybe one that just ate a village of trolls. I think I saw a picture like that once. He popped the little trolls into his mouth like they were chips."

Sam studied the castles. "I'm psyched," he said. "For

the sightseeing, not the troll eating. And that's saying something, because I like eating."

"I think we know that," I said. "I guess we need to get tickets to go in."

Caroline sighed. "We don't have to go in, do we? We can just hang out here and mock all the tourists walking by. I mean, unless you want to." She said it like it was a ridiculously lame idea.

What can I say? I mean, of course I want to go in. I'm in London to see the sights, DUH!

I needed to make this more interesting than an average field trip.

I got an idea.

"Mocking the tourists sounds superfun," I said to Caroline. "But I thought maybe you'd want to see the Crown Jewels. And, Ellie, I thought you might want to see the ghosts that haunt this place. Sam, the brochure I read said they have an assortment of royal chocolates in the gift shop."

"I'd forgotten that the Crown Jewels were here," Caroline said, reconsidering. "We didn't see them on our school trip."

Ellie said, "We didn't see any ghosts then either. They probably don't take schoolkids to the truly ghostly parts of the Tower, eh?"

"What are we waiting for?" Sam asked.

Yay, me! I had gotten them a little interested.

We passed through the stone archway, on top of which was an iron gate that would be dropped to protect the royal court from threats.

Inside the Tower walls my eyes feasted on the old stone buildings. I imagined ladies in layered lacy dresses, maybe a poor fellow locked in a stockade, and a stray dog scampering for a scrap of bread.

We took a long bridge that passed over a grassy path. I overheard a tour guide, who was dressed in a yeoman's tunic, saying that the plush greenway was once a moat. I took lots of pictures.

"The deep water was like a security system," Sam added. "It was probably filled with man-eating fish."

"Now, *that's* cool," Ellie said. "Too bad they filled it in."

Caroline's mobile rang. She answered it and spoke for just a second in hushed tones that I couldn't decipher. "It was Stepmummy. She got the picture, and noticed J.J. wasn't all smiles. I assured her you were having a grand old time." Then she asked, "So, where are the jewels?"

I looked at the map. "For the Jewel House we need to go this way."

"Then let's head over there." Caroline hooked her

arm into mine and walked with me like we were Dorothy and the lion parading down the yellow brick road. (I would be the lion in that scene.) I was continuing to follow the directions, when I saw something that I thought Ellie would be interested in. It had that horror-movie feel to it. "See this tower?" I asked her. "They call it the Bloody Tower."

"Awesome," Ellie said. "Let's go in."

"Oh, yes! Let's," Caroline said excitedly, too excitedly? Or was she actually getting into this?

We walked inside the Bloody Tower. A cool feeling of death and despair was everywhere as I followed the signs and led the group up a narrow spiral staircase surrounded by stone walls. Velvet ropes blocked us from a small room that held only a few pieces of furniture: an ornate wooden chair, a writing desk, a small wooden bed against the wall. There was light from just one square window.

"I don't see any ghosts," Ellie said. "What a rip-off."

We followed the gloomy corridors, whose silence felt very haunted. The corridors were narrow and bendy. Occasionally there was a mirror in the corner, angled so that you could see if someone was coming from the other direction. I didn't like the eerie feeling in this place. I walked fast until I made it outside to the warm sun.

I continued walking in the direction of the jewels,

but then I saw the Tower Green. I stopped and stared at the square patch of grass. It was smaller than I'd imagined, considering what went on there.

"What is it?" Sam asked me. "What's wrong?"

"This is the Tower Green. It's where they held public executions," I said.

Caroline said, "That's what the medieval times were all about. Maybe it's novel to you because Columbus hadn't even discovered America yet. But we know all about it."

I didn't know what to say; this *was* new to me. Maybe they'd seen it all before, but I hadn't.

Caroline looked like maybe she realized her comment was insensitive, and tried to gloss it over. "But that's why you're here, isn't it?" She smiled. "To see our wonderful history."

I stared at the Green. "I especially like Anne Boleyn's story. It's so romantic and tragic," I said.

"I love romance," Gordo said.

"I love tragic," Ellie said.

"Go on," Caroline. "Tell us what you know about her."

I was a little apprehensive because I couldn't tell if she really wanted to hear the story. "Well, King Henry was married to Catherine when he fell madly in love with Anne, one of her lady's maids. Henry and Anne married, and their love was true and deep. They had a daughter who later became queen. But after they had been married for several years, King Henry began courting Lady Jane Seymour and he wanted to marry her. So that the new marriage could be legal, he told everyone that Anne had bewitched him to make him fall in love with her. Anne was locked away in the Tower and eventually executed—in this exact spot right here." A chill went through my entire body, and for a moment no one spoke.

"Positively gruesome," Ellie finally said with a sparkle in her eye.

I took a picture of the grassy area. "Here, let me get a picture of you on the Green," Caroline said, and took my phone. "Now smile really big." She clicked the picture, handed the phone back to me, and said, "Send that to the mums too."

I did.

"Now, how about the jewels?" Caroline asked again.

We entered the narrow stone corridor of the Jewel House. It was dark and damp. Security cameras along the halls reminded me that modern surveillance was in use, not that we were planning to do any dress-up or trampolining.

The main room that housed the jewels was also

guarded by security men, the no-nonsense-no-tunic kind.

Caroline got dangerously close to one of the glass cases that shielded from potential theft crowns and scepters adorned with enormous gems. A guard cleared his throat, and Caroline stepped back.

I went to click a picture, and the guard told me I couldn't in this room.

I said, "I would love a time machine so that I could go back and see these actually being worn at a big celebration with dancing and live music and court jesters." As soon as I said it, I wished I hadn't. Caroline didn't think about things like time machines.

Apparently Gordo did. "And knights with swords and shields."

Caroline said, "But I'm not interested in living without air-conditioning or cell phones or Jacuzzi tubs or TV. No thanks. I'll pass."

"I don't need a time machine," Ellie said. "The MoviePlex takes me to all sorts of places in time. That's the same MoviePlex that's showing *Bloodsucking Zombies* at four o'clock, which we can make if we leave *right now*." She sang "right now."

"Yes!" Caroline said. "I mean, as long as J.J. is okay with that. I think you're going to absolutely LOVE this picture. It's all the rage."

"Okay," I agreed, and I liked that Caroline had checked with me. She had been totally nice and attentive to me today, and initially she hadn't even wanted to come.

"Right after we check out the gift shop," Ellie said. "I never leave anywhere without a souvenir."

"Fine," Caroline agreed. "We'll all get souvenirs."

Gordo bought a little knight figurine, Sam grabbed some chocolate, and even Caroline got a few postcards. I chose a London bus key chain to put in my new purse.

Ellie got a three-foot-tall pencil with a big crown eraser, and a tiara that she wore out of the store.

Outside the Tower walls, we were back in modern London; I followed the gang underground via stairs in the sidewalk. In medieval times this might have led to a dungeon, but today I suspected it went to something like a subway. Not like I had ever actually been on a subway, but I'd seen them on TV and in movies.

"This is the Tube," Sam said.

The Tube? How British. I imagined myself in a New York subway one day and saying to the person I was with, *It's nice, but it's not like the Tube in London. Have you ever been on the Tube? Well, I have, and I can tell you all about it, if you'd like.* Or maybe I'd be back at school and someone from our lame school paper would interview me about this trip and I could say something like, *Well, we took the Tube from sight to sight. Don't you know what that is? Well, let me explain . . .*

The walls were white, with different-colored stripes indicating the routes. Sam seemed to know which underground train to get on. I sat on a hard plastic seat. Ellie was in front of me, holding on to a metal pole. The train took off through the tunnel, which was kinda like an underground tube. I guessed that was where it got its name. The train moved so fast that Ellie kept bumping into me.

"Sorry," she said. She took her phone and clicked four or five pictures of everyone acting silly. Then she held it out and took one of herself in her tiara, which she hadn't taken off. "I'll text these to you so you'll have them." She frowned. "Drat! No signal down here."

We emerged from underground, and I felt my phone vibrating in my new purse. I looked at it. I figured it was the pictures Ellie had just sent, but it wasn't. "Oh no," I said. "It's Sebastian. He wants his pages at five o'clock instead of eight."

"Can he do that?" Ellie asked. "Just change the time?"

"No," Sam said. "He can't. Tell him he's a twit and we'll get him the pages as agreed."

I texted Sebastian back, leaving out the part about

the twit and writing much more politely than any of them would have.

He immediately replied.

"What did he say?" Gordo asked.

"It's just a link." I clicked it, and it went to an online video. I held it out for the others to see. They had to crowd around me. Sam's cheek practically touched mine, and I felt the wisps of the longish part of his hair on my face.

The video began to play. The background was Daphne's. The video was familiar. You could clearly see two people in costumes, jumping on a trampoline. There were no faces, but I could hear my own voice and Caroline's.

"That looks like fun," Ellie said. "Can we do that?"

"Blast it!" Caroline groaned.

16

We sat on the curb outside the MoviePlex. Sam tapped out words that Gordo dictated based on the printouts he had. Gordo also told him where to add a citation.

Ellie fidgeted and kept looking at her watch. "It's almost four o'clock. I'm going to miss the previews. I hate missing the previews. Can't you go any faster?"

Sam picked up his hand-phone and looked at Ellie. "It's the Shut Your Piehole Factory; they want to talk to you," he said.

She closed her mouth and huffed over to Caroline

and started imitating Sam on his finger-phone. Caroline sent Ellie to buy tickets. I really hoped this movie would involve popcorn. I wouldn't mind a hot dog, but that might be too much to hope for.

Finally Sam said, "Okay, it's sent to the pastry jerk. We overachieved, my friend. Two hundred and fifty-six words." He gave Gordo a high five.

Ellie rushed us through the theater. I passed a poster for *Bloodsucking Zombies*. It was a gruesome image of a walking-dead person with blood dripping from his mouth. I noticed it was rated "15." A quick glance of the other movies and ratings told me that meant it was for kids fifteen and older. A little beat of excitement pulsed through my veins. Ellie handed me a ticket. I guess she'd passed for fifteen, which wasn't really surprising. "My treat," she said.

I thanked her.

I sat between Ellie and Sam. After only a second, Sam got up and left. "BRB," he whispered.

Ellie said, "You know I started 'BRB'?"

"Yeah?" I asked.

She nodded. I think she believed that she had started the abbreviation, but I didn't think so.

The theater darkened, and a few previews later, blood started splattering everywhere.

Ellie was entranced. Something on the ground caught my eye. Her feet were glowing. She saw that I was staring. "Glow-in-the-dark socks," she said. "Very popular."

"Really?" I had never heard of them. I glanced down the row. Gordo's feet were kicked up onto the chair in front of him, and a smile covered his face. I think Caroline was checking her watch. It was like she always wanted to be somewhere else, but her friends were all here. It didn't make sense to me. In some ways I wanted to be like her—she was so pretty and had cool clothes and everyone wanted to be around her. But I didn't think she was that nice to her friends. She'd been really nice to me all day, but it felt different than it had at Daphne's. It was like she was . . . *acting.*

Sam came back with a bucket of popcorn and a mega-huge soda.

"Help yourself," he whispered into my ear.

"Did you hear my stomach growling?" I whispered back.

"No, but I can only imagine after hanging out with those guys all day."

"Why don't they eat?" I asked.

He said, "Too busy, I think."

Ellie shh-ed us. Sam and I stared at the screen with our hands occasionally meeting in the bucket. I had to think about something other than the blood and guts on the screen for a second:

- I was in London, staying in a mansion.
- I'd just come from seeing the Crown Jewels.
- I now sat at a movie, sharing popcorn with a totally cute British boy.
- Oh, and I had on hot new clothes and makeup, and had a great new hairdo.

This had been a pretty successful trip so far, except for being blackmailed by some guy to do his homework. And that there were videos of me (faceless, thankfully) online in connection with a robbery.

Yup. I'd say smashingly successful so far.

The movie was terrible, but the popcorn was good. I learned a new English word that I thought maybe I would try to use while I was here.

They sat through all the credits. When the house-lights came on, they still didn't get up.

"That was so good," Ellie said. "I totally cannot wait to see it again. Did you see that bloke's fingers go into the blender? He didn't even feel it. I think I want to be a zombie when I die."

"Too true," Gordo said. "But with better hair."

Caroline said, "That picture had better win some major awards. I love Riley Goodwin; he is so cute."

Sam asked, "Which one was he?"

"Are you kidding?" Ellie asked. "You're just having a laugh, Sam, right? Everyone knows who Riley Goodwin is. The hot zombie. The one who never wore a shirt."

"How can a zombie be hot?" Sam asked. "I mean, they're dead. They must smell terrible, and random body parts just fall off and tumble to the ground."

Gordo said, "Just 'cause they're dead doesn't mean they should completely neglect their hygiene, does it? Half of them had bugs crawling out of their ears or nose or eyes. That's not hot. But even I have to admit that Riley Goodwin is a good-looking guy."

Then Sam held his thumb and pinky to his ear and mouth like he was making a phone call. "Hi," he said. "I am looking for the Hot Zombie Club. Can you help me? Oh, you can't because zombies aren't hot? Okay, thanks. That's what I thought too."

Ellie shooed Sam and continued talking to Caroline. "Do you think he owns a shirt that isn't ripped to shreds?"

"I hope not," Caroline said. She looked at her watch. "Latte?"

Gordo said, "The sooner the better."

Caroline asked me, "You think your mom will be okay with us stopping for a warm beverage, or will you miss too much sightseeing?" She sounded like it was a totally normal question, but it was mean, right?

"I think she'll be okay with that."

We walked to a small coffee shop next door. Gordo, Ellie, and Caroline all shared a sandwich. Sam and I each got our own scone and passed on the latte.

"I suppose we'll head to the train, and we can do yet another fabulously touristy thing tomorrow," Caroline said. I wasn't sure she really meant that touristy things were fabulous. "That new reality show about the cooking club is on tonight, right? I cannot wait to see it. They're going to have a live online chat during the show."

Sam said, "It's only seven o'clock. And it's not raining. It's a good night to go to the Eye. Is that on your list, J.J.?"

"Oh, yeah," I said. "I really want to ride that big Ferris wheel."

Caroline exhaled like this was terribly inconvenient for her reality TV schedule. She pushed out a smile. "Maybe we should save it for tomorrow?"

"Why don't you stay here," Gordo said. "Look, they

have a telly." He indicated an ancient TV in the corner near the cappuccino machine. "We'll come back and get you when we're done. Your stepmummy didn't say you had to be in every picture. We'll take J.J. and we'll text the photo."

Hmmm, I thought. *It might even be more fun without her.*

"Fine," she said. "Ellie and I will hang here while you ride that wheel."

Ellie pouted. "I sorta want to go."

"That's just fab," Caroline said. "Then we'll all go, won't we?"

17

London was lit up under the night sky like a perfect postcard. I was looking up and wondering which light was Pluto, when I saw the London Eye in the distance.

A regular Ferris wheel from a Wilmington carnival was like a dwarf planet compared to this gigantic wheel.

Once we were right under it, Ellie looked up. "It looks even more massive up close, doesn't it?"

"I suppose we should get a photo for the mums," Caroline said. She tapped a passerby to take it. "Smile big, J.J.," she said as we posed.

I looked at the photo on the screen, and it showed the five of us but didn't capture the wheel or the River Thames behind us. "You can't tell where we are," I said.

"We can get a better shot from up top," Sam said.

We moved up in line, which Gordo called the queue. Caroline said, "Let me guess. You read all about the London Eye before you came."

"Yes," I said, embarrassed.

"Please enlighten us," she said.

This felt like a pop quiz for which I didn't know the answers. I looked down at the brochure as if I needed it to give me the information, which I didn't. "It was built to be the biggest Ferris wheel in the world, and it was until two bigger ones were built, one in China and one in Singapore."

Caroline looked up. "Bigger than this?"

It seemed that I knew something that Caroline hadn't learned on a field trip.

Our turn came up faster than I expected, even though the Eye turned very slowly. The Eye didn't even stop to let us on. We walked onto the clear plastic capsule that was like a big bubble with a long bench down the middle.

"How long does this take?" Ellie asked.

"A half hour for a rotation," I said.

We were off the ground and above the river. The panoramic view of the city was beautiful and amazing, and I sent my mom and dad a mental thank-you for letting me go on this trip. "Oh my gosh," I said. "Look at the lights of Big Ben and the Palace of Westminster. I want to go there so badly."

My four new friends soaked in the view. "It really is spectacular," Gordo said. Ellie took my phone and asked another capsule passenger to take our picture. The person didn't speak English but understood what she was asking.

Under her breath Caroline said, "You'd think the least these people could do is unbutton the top of their oxford shirts. Maybe the top button is in style in their country, but not here."

The tourists showed no sign of hearing or understanding her, thankfully. That would've been so embarrassing.

We stood with our backs to the capsule's glass wall so that Big Ben was in the picture. It came out great. I texted the proof of our stop at the London Eye to our moms.

"I wonder why they call it Big Ben," Ellie said.

How can she not know this? "The biggest chiming bell of the clock tower is called Ben and gives the tower its nickname."

"Why 'Ben,' and not 'Bob' or 'Burt'?" Caroline asked.

"There is the name of a politician named Benjamin Somebody inscribed on the bell," I said.

"You seem to know a lot about this stuff," Caroline said. "What else do you know about the clock?"

I thought she was joking, maybe setting me up to be mocked, but her face showed no indication that she was anything but serious. "Well, it's the only tower with four faces of a clock. And it's known for its accuracy. It's been lit and has kept good time for a hundred and fifty years. During the First and Second World Wars the lights were turned off to protect it from attacks. Also, only UK residents can go in."

"Bummer, eh?" Caroline asked. "We'll just have to focus all our fun time elsewhere. I'm sure you have other places we can visit on that list of yours."

"I'd love to get a picture in front of it," I said, even though I knew it would be an unpopular idea.

"Sure thing," Sam said on behalf of his friends.

Caroline's glare said that he did not have the authority to make a commitment like that on her behalf. "Maybe we can fit it in one day," she said coldly.

Needless to say, we didn't get that picture.

18

The next day at breakfast Mrs. Littleton asked us, "Where are y'all going today?" She looked like she had already been to yoga.

I said, "I was thinking Madame Tussauds."

I caught Caroline puff out an annoyed exhale. "Bril," she said with a smile that I didn't believe.

"Maybe I'll come along," Mrs. Littleton said. "Just let me get a quick shower."

"Oh," Caroline said, looking at her watch. "I wish we

could wait, but we were supposed to pick up the others about five minutes ago."

"Oh, drat! Well, have fun," Mrs. Littleton said. "Before ya go, I just wanna talk to Caroline for one smidgen of a second."

Caroline followed Mrs. Littleton to the hallway. I could hear a hushed conversation. As promised, they returned to the kitchen in a smidgen of a second. "Will we see you for dinner?" Mrs. Littleton asked.

"Unlikely," Caroline said. "We'll probably go to some London icon; you know, to make sure J.J. has a superepic time here in London."

It was amazing how her mom kept trusting us. I never had this much freedom at home.

Liam was waiting to drive us to the train station. I was already hungry because the berries and tea from breakfast hadn't been enough to fill me. I couldn't wait to see Sam, both because I was starting to really like hanging out with him—okay, so maybe I was starting to like him—and because he'd be into getting a snack with me.

From two blocks away I could see the huge green dome. I knew from my pre-travel research it was Madame Tussauds, the famous wax museum. It's the home of tons of wax figures of famous people, like Tom Cruise,

Angelina Jolie, politicians, athletes, and any other star you could imagine. It's been visited by famous people and tourists for almost two hundred years.

"Oh, blast," Caroline said. "Look at this queue." We were in a long line of people waiting to get in. She looked at her phone. "There's no new videos uploaded, so those pages must've met the pastry pest's standards."

"Did you say 'pastry'?" Sam asked. "Because I think there's a shop right around the corner. It's not as good as Lively's, but it's all right."

"Sounds like something we should check out," I said.

Ellie said, "We'll get in the queue while you get something to eat."

Sam and I crossed the street, which is harder than you'd think when people are driving on the wrong side of the road.

Sam asked for two scones. I ate it as slowly as I could, which was kinda fast. It really hit the spot.

We rejoined the gang, who had inched up in line a bit.

Gordo said, "Let's work on the next set of pages now. We can't do anything else while we're standing here."

Ellie said, "Give me the Pad-i, and I'll type today."

"Pad-i?" I asked.

"Yeah. Like 'Pad Thai,'" she said.

I asked, "What's wrong with 'iPad'?"

"I thought it might be fun to change it. You know, see if it catches on," she said. "Who knows, maybe I'll start a whole new trend. You know I was the first to use 'BTW'?"

"I didn't know that," I said. Ellie nodded, confirming that it was her. I wondered if Ellie could single-handedly rename the Apple suite of products. I doubted it, but I admired her for trying.

"You go for it," Gordo encouraged Ellie.

Caroline examined her nails.

Ellie fished the tiara from the Tower of London out of her purse and set it on her spiky head. She checked her reflection in the museum's tinted windows.

Caroline looked at her. "Seriously?"

"What?" Ellie asked. "Don't you like it? I wonder why women stopped wearing them."

"Because they look dumb," Caroline said.

Ellie didn't take it off. I thought maybe she was trying to start another trend. I loved that Ellie wore it even though Caroline had just said it was dumb.

The line inched forward.

"Are you a good typer?" I asked Ellie while she touched the iPad screen, which Gordo held for her.

"Not really, but I like to do it. I'm not a good tap

dancer either, but I like to do that, too." She clomped her feet around and smiled.

Caroline's foot was tapping, but it was much less enthusiastic than Ellie's. "Let's get a photo now," Caroline said, "so we can take off quickly when we're done." I wondered why she was in such a big hurry.

Sam asked the lady in front of us to take our picture. Caroline once again reminded me to smile big. I looked at the picture on the small LCD screen before sending it to the mums.

Caroline said, "We've got the shot. Do you wanna skip this and just go see the zombie picture again? This place gives me the creeps."

"But a zombie movie doesn't?" asked Sam.

"That's different," Caroline said. "That's Hollywood. This place is, like, actual spookiness right here in front of us."

"Too true," Ellie added. "That's what I like about it. Can you imagine if you'd been locked in *here* overnight instead of Daphne's?"

"Shhh!" Everyone shushed her.

"Sorry. But *that* would've been a bomb."

Gordo said, "I haven't been here since I was a kid. I liked it then, and I wanna see it again."

"Same," Ellie said.

"Do they have food?" Sam asked.

"Yes!" we all assured him.

"Speaking of food," I said, "if you ever want a lemon tart again, we should work on those pages."

It seemed like everyone had ignored Caroline's suggestion to go to the movie. Her toe tapping and watch-looking indicated that she didn't like that, but for some reason she didn't make a big deal about it.

Sam read a few lines from a printout he still had in his pocket, and Ellie used the touch screen to type. Every few words she said "Oops" or "Wait a sec."

And then, just to tease her, Sam would talk really fast. "Slow down, Sam," Ellie told him, but he sped up again, even faster. Sam dictated, "Pluto was a planet until recently, when astronomers decided it was too small and stripped it of that title."

"That's good," Ellie said. "I am totally writing that—stripped it—it's very dramatic and really makes you feel bad for the sad little dwarf planet. Kinda like Sebastian is a dwarf person."

I admired that even though they were waiting in line for some touristy thing, writing a school paper for someone else—an annoying bully who spit in their tarts—they were still having fun. I really liked these guys. I looked at Caroline fiddling with her phone, and I didn't understand why they'd want to be friends with *her*. But I did understand why she would want to be friends with *them*.

Once again Ellie was nagging Sam to slow down, when I heard something familiar. With a start, I realized it was my own voice coming from the phone of the girl behind us in line.

Motioning for everyone in our group to be quiet, I tilted my head toward the girl.

We heard Caroline's voice too—and lots of laughing.

It was the trampoline video clip that Sebastian had uploaded.

19

The girl behind us in line, the one chomping on her chewing gum, held her phone out enough for us to listen and watch. It was the news reporters again:

The anchor named Skye said, *"The recent theft at Daphne's remains unsolved, but it's believed that these two people are responsible."*

They flashed a still photo of our feet midjump.

"As you can see, there are no images of the suspects' faces. But from the voices, it's assumed to be two girls—an American and a Brit. Police have reviewed the surveillance

cameras from the night in question, but since the storm knocked out the electricity, there is no recording."

The reporter named Cole asked, "Skye, what about a backup generator? Surely a store as high-tech as Daphne's has a backup system?"

"Indeed. They do have a generator, which was disconnected. The Daphne's security team said the heist was well thought-out, because these girls chose a night when a storm killed the electricity, and they also knew how to disconnect a generator."

"They sound like smart and experienced thieves," Cole said. "What happens next?"

"The authorities will comb the videos before power was lost to see if they find a pair of girls matching these feet," Skye said, and the screen filled with the shot of our feet again.

"Can you believe it?" Bubble Gum said. "They recorded themselves and then put it on the Internet. It's like they *want* to get caught."

Then her friend with a pierced nose said, "Why would they want that? They'll probably go up the river if they get caught."

"I can't imagine it will take that long to identify them," Bubble Gum said.

"Then what?" Pierced Nose asked.

"Bring them in for questioning, I guess," Bubble Gum

said. "I'll make you a bet that they have the American-British robber pair in custody before morning."

Pierced Nose said, "No way. The police aren't that good. I'll take that wager."

"What shall we bet?" Bubble Gum asked. "Tickets to the Riley Goodwin picture?"

"YES!" Pierced Nose agreed. They shook on it.

I whispered, "What are we going to do?"

Gordo said, "All right. Starting now you're not American, J.J."

Ellie asked, "How about Chinese? Can you do a Chinese accent?"

"That's a good idea," I said. "But even if I could, I don't think I can *look* Chinese."

"You haven't tried."

Sam said, "Why don't you just be English? From Manchester."

"I guess I could try that," I said.

"In the meantime it wouldn't hurt for you to lie low," Sam said.

Caroline said, "We're standing in the queue at a museum. It doesn't get much lower than this."

"I know!" Ellie raised her hand like an eight-year-old in school. She waited for Caroline's acknowledgment to allow her to talk. "One word. 'Disguises.' I am the best at disguises. We had a costume party at my school, and I won the prize for the best costume. I went as a royal guard with a homemade hat. I made the hat with pillow stuffing and painted it black. It was, like, four feet tall. Tell her how awesome it was, Sam."

"It was actually quite good," Sam agreed.

Ellie said, "I thought everyone was going to make their own and wear them to school the next day, but it didn't catch on that way. That's the thing with starting new fads, sometimes they catch on and sometimes they don't—"

"Anyway," Caroline interrupted. "Back in the real world I suppose a little camouflage wouldn't be a totally awful idea."

"True," Gordo agreed.

Ellie said, "I don't want to totally freak you out, but look." She pointed to two policemen coming down the street. "Duck!"

Caroline bent down as if she was tying her shoe, which was silly because she was wearing boots with zippers. "Stop pointing!"

I stuck my head into my purse like I was looking for something very important that was way down at the bottom in the corner. I continued to hunt until Ellie said, "They're gone. You can climb out of your designer bag now. I've never actually seen someone try to fit inside a handbag. You gave it a good go. Let me try."

She took my purse and bent her head down into it but didn't get very far. "You're better at it. One time I tried to see if my foot would fit into an orange juice container. My foot was smaller back then, of course. I got my foot in but couldn't get it out, and since I couldn't walk with it on my foot, I had to hop around until my dad could saw it off—the plastic orange container, that is, not my foot, obviously, because I still have it. See."

She held up her leg and showed us her foot, like it would be news to us that her foot was still there. Caroline's eyes said she was irritated by Ellie's moronic behavior, but I got a laugh out of it—something I definitely needed at the moment.

"We know all about the ol' foot-in-the-orange-juice-container story," Caroline said. "But right now we have something to take care of. Can you boys stay in line and save our places?"

Gordo studied how far we had left to go before we got into the wax museum. "You'd better be quick."

As we girls set out to buy disguises, I overheard Bubble Gum say, "I wish that was me. How awesome would it be to stay in Daphne's overnight? Those two chicks are my heroes."

She was talking about me! Boring old me was her hero!

Then Pierced Nose said, "You aren't kidding. I'd love to have an exciting night like that, except I wouldn't steal anything."

"Come on," Ellie said, and she ushered us away.

"How are we gonna get out of this?" I asked. "My parents are going to be superangry if they find out the police are looking for me."

"We need two things," Caroline said. "Disguises, and to get those videos from the Tart Fart so that he can't upload anything else to the Internet, or turn anything over to the police."

Ellie was laughing so hard that she had to hold herself up against the brick wall of the building we were going to walk into. "Tart Fart! That's a good one, Car. I LOVE it."

"Caroline," she corrected Ellie.

"Ahhh." She exhaled and caught her breath back. "Right. Sorry about that." She was slightly more serious as she held the door to the Shamrock Boutique open for us. "Maybe if you apologize for breaking in and stealing the electronics—"

"We didn't break in!" Caroline said loud enough to draw attention from the four customers and store lady.

"And." She lowered her voice but said very firmly, "We. Didn't. Steal. Anything."

"Jeez," Ellie whispered. "You don't need to yell about it. Okay, you have five minutes for the ultimate disguises. I'll be over here by the earrings for free consultations."

"Why are you whispering?" I asked.

"Because I don't want her to yell at me again."

I went right for a soft pink wool cap with a really big flower pin affixed to it.

"Yes, that is perfect for you," Ellie whispered very loudly across the store. I looked at a rack of sunglasses, touched a few, and chose a pair. "Yes," she hissed again. She could whisper pretty loudly. "Those shades would be perfect for you."

"You can stop whispering," I said across the small boutique.

"Oh, good. I didn't like it."

The sunglasses were like two postage-stamp-size lenses held together by a thin metal frame.

"Really? You like these?" I put them on.

"Totally bohemian," she said. She added a feathery scarf and wrapped it around my neck several times.

Caroline had tucked her hair under a red French beret, put on a well-worn denim jacket, lifted the collar up to cover the bottom of her face, and added her big white sunglasses with the rhinestones that she already had in her purse.

Ellie slid a credit card across the counter; it amazed me the way these girls could charge stuff. Before we left the boutique, something caught my eye. A woman working there was piercing a little girl's ears. The little girl was squeezing her eyes shut and hugging a stuffed bear into her belly, when there was a *POP!* The store lady shot an earring into her ear with a handheld gun gadget.

"Are you done?" the little girl asked.

"All done. That didn't hurt, did it?"

"No, uh-uh."

If she could do it, so could I. I'd never be able to get the second hole at home.

"Wait!" I called to Ellie and Caroline. Then I asked the store lady, "How fast can you give me second holes?"

The store lady popped her gun. "Less than a second per ear."

I sat and pointed to a pair of earrings. The little girl handed me her bear. The store lady loaded the gun, and *POP!* She reloaded, and *POP!* And I was done.

On the sidewalk Ellie touched my back and my sides, and patted my purse. "What are you doing?" I asked as she did the same thing to Caroline.

140

"Just making sure you didn't steal anything from that nice little store," she teased.

"Oh MIIIIIGod! Do you listen?" Caroline asked.

A few minutes later, after Gordo oohed and aahed over my earrings and our disguises, we entered Madame Tussauds on the lush carpet and followed the path to the first display—a random selection of US presidents.

Ellie stared. "Blimey! They look so real. I want to kiss one of them."

"NO KISSING!" a voice behind us bellowed.

A figure stood perfectly still in the corner. Ellie walked toward her. "She looks like an actual person." Ellie moved her face very close to the guard's to examine her.

"I AM a real person," the guard said, shocking Ellie so much that she fell to the ground.

She stood up and rubbed her butt. "That hurt," she said.

After I took a picture of the guard, we moved to the next display. It was the cast of *Bloodsucking Zombies*, dressed up like they were at an awards show.

Ellie said, "I just love them. I wish they were here right now, because I want to meet them."

"Me too," Caroline said. She continued to lead the

way past countless wax celebrities. She stopped at a display of people I didn't recognize. It was a group of ladies from Victorian times standing in front of Madame Tussauds in the evening. The wax lampposts looked like they were lit with oil, and the sidewalk appeared to be cobblestone.

Caroline's mouth hung open. "Their dresses are incredible."

Gordo read a plaque that was just inside a velvet rope keeping us back far enough so our breath wouldn't touch the figures. "Says here that these gowns are all handmade. Guess who made them?"

"Who?" Sam asked, chewing a soft pretzel that had materialized in his hand.

"Daphne," Caroline guessed.

"Yup," Sam said. "It says that she started her fashion empire by first hand-sewing party dresses that she sold at the front of Madame Tussauds. Then she was hired as the official seamstress of the museum. Her dresses became so popular that she expanded her business and it continued to grow. Her wax likeness is in the next hall."

"Let's see it," Ellie said.

"Can we get a photo first?" I asked.

Sam nudged me. "Manchester."

"I dare say," I said. "Might we snap a photo in front of these dear mannequins?"

Sam wiped the longish hairs out of his face. "Um, we'll work on that."

We passed several displays until we got to one of a young Daphne, who was plainly dressed, no makeup. She held a little girl's party dress in each hand—one red, one blue. They were elaborately decorated with every embellishment imaginable—beads, sequins, and lace. The plaque said, MS. DAPHNE WHITWORTH, FUTURE PRESIDENT AND CEO OF DAPHNE'S.

"She looks so ordinary. I expected someone far more chic," Caroline said. "You know, my dad knew her before she died. Her daughter is in charge of the store now. My stepmum claims to be her yoga friend, but I don't believe her."

Gordo said, "It's possible. My mum knows her. Her name is Sophie."

"Here's a picture of her." Sam held out his phone.

We all looked over his shoulder. "I think I'm in love," Gordo said.

"Me too," I almost said. She was dressed casually, in jeans and cute sneakers. She was a natural beauty. Of all the fashion looks I'd seen so far in London, this was my favorite. It was like she wasn't even trying to be beautiful. She just was. That was exactly the style of pretty I wanted to be.

Gordo stared at the phone's screen. "Sophie Whitworth. I'd love to meet her!"

"So would I," Caroline said. "My dad, as you know, has connections, and he hasn't ever been able to get us a meeting. She leads a very private life."

"If your faces get identified from the surveillance cameras, you might be meeting her," Sam said.

"Where are we going now?" Ellie asked. "All I want to do is soak my tired tootsies in a hot tub and get my toes done."

"Sounds good," Gordo said.

"*Oui,*" Caroline said. "Let's do that."

I had never actually had my toes done. If this was a week of adventure, maybe I should be open to exploring the concept of pretty toes to match my new look.

"What about Pluto?" Ellie asked.

"We can work on it there while our toes are drying," Gordo said.

"I know the perfect place," Caroline said. "No one will recognize us. J.J., you are going to LOVE this."

Something strange, and wonderful, had happened

over the last two days. Was Caroline finally starting to care about making sure I had a good time? I didn't know what that stuff was that she'd said to Ellie, but thanks to our adventure in Daphne's, maybe she was finally starting to like me.

20

We arrived at Salon London. It was a simple shop with three mani stations and three pedi chairs. The windows were covered with heavy, dusty drapes. Incense sticks burned on the floor next to a little Buddha statue. We were the only customers in the place.

Sam said, "I think I'm gonna go find a sandwich."

"What?" Gordo asked. "You're not going to get your feet soaked?"

"I'll pass," he said. "J.J., do you want to go look for a sandwich with me?"

"Actually," I said, "I'd like to check this out."

"Fine, I'll get you some chips. These girls will go all day without eating. And I'm including Gordo in that statement."

"I heard that!" Gordo said with a smile.

A man came out and gestured to the chairs. Before long, Caroline and I were soaking our feet. Ellie and Gordo were nearby with their fingers dangling in bowls of soapy water. I didn't realize how tired my feet were until a small woman wearing long false eyelashes started rubbing them. It felt heavenly. Now I knew why Ellie wanted to do this.

Another woman walked around carrying a selection of nail polish colors. I chose a light pink. Caroline casually shook her head. I chose again—red—and showed it to her for her approval. She shook her head again. This went on until I held up a dark blue.

She chose gold, and Ellie black. Gordo was going with clear.

After an amazing foot massage with scented lotion, I sat with my feet under a fan. Caroline switched places with Gordo. I opted to skip the manicure because I was starting to worry about money, and I didn't think I could sell this to my mom and dad as an emergency. I flipped through a magazine until Sam returned. He held a grease-stained paper bag.

"Chips," he said.

I opened the bag. It was filled with french fries. "What's on them?"

"Salt and vinegar."

It didn't sound good, but I was hungry and I had mentally declared that I was going to give everything a try. . . . Well, not anything raw or gross.

Hesitantly I tried one.

"Quite good, eh?" Sam asked.

"It is. Thanks."

He sat next to me and looked at my toes. "Blue?"

"Caroline picked it out. Do you like it?"

He shrugged in a way that said *I don't really care but I want to be polite, so*: "Sure."

"How are we on today's word count for Sebastian's paper?"

"Still about eighty short."

"We can do that in no time," I said.

He reached into his back pocket for a rolled-up bunch of paper. "Be my guest. You just tell me what to type."

I scanned the pages for another tidbit or two about Pluto's composition. That was all we really needed for eighty words. "How about the idea that Pluto is one of thousands of objects that make up a ring far, far away from the sun. Pluto is the largest of these objects that form a belt in the universe."

He typed. "Okay, that's good." He tapped more words than I had said, obviously trying to stretch it out to eighty words. "Almost there," he said.

"Okay, use this. 'It is similar in composition to the other objects in the belt.' And 'made mostly of ice.' You have to footnote that section with this reference." I pointed to the website name on the paper.

"Read it to me," he said.

I gave him the website information that was in the top margin of the paper.

"Perfect. Done." He sent the pages. "The little poop gets it early today."

The footnote gave me an idea. "Are you making a bibliography?"

"Yes. Of course. Don't you use bibliographies in America?"

"Duh. Yes. But that just gave me an idea of how we might be able to rat out Sebastian." I explained my idea to Sam.

"I like it," he said.

"Do you think we can do it?"

"Maybe," he said. He reached into my chip bag and

put a handful into his mouth at once. I took some too but only ate one at a time.

"How many places are left on your list?" Gordo asked me.

"I want to see the Royal Mews, Westminster Abbey, Buckingham Palace, the London Dungeon, the Changing of the Guard, and Saint Paul's Cathedral."

Caroline called over from the pedicure chair, "Isn't that a little ambitious for three days?"

"We have nights, too," Sam said.

I excused myself to use the ladies' room. I left the bathroom door open a crack while I washed and dried my hands. I could see Caroline and Ellie in a serious conversation. Caroline's back was to me, but I could see her using her arms to talk.

I heard her saying, ". . . so we're spending our entire week standing in queues. Could it get any more boring? I swear that if Stepmum hadn't promised me a trip to Jamaica as long as J.J. had a great time, I'd bag this whole thing. You know the Mash-Up concert is tonight? And we're not going to it. I mean, really? I am bored out of my blooming mind!"

Caroline had just confirmed all of my greatest fears. I suddenly felt like an imposition and a bother. Worst of all, my de-bored-ification plan clearly wasn't working.

21

Ellie looked over Caroline's shoulder and noticed me.

"Is that true?" I asked angrily. I held back the tears that were coming. I did NOT want her to see me cry. I couldn't believe that I'd thought she'd actually been having fun. I'd totally fallen for her act. She didn't want to be doing any of this, and she didn't like me. She was pretending in exchange for a trip to Jamaica.

Caroline turned around.

I said, "I mean, is it true for all of you?" Ellie was staring at the floor, Gordo dried his nails, and Sam ate a black and white cookie that he'd gotten from somewhere. I didn't know where, but I wished I had one.

"Have you all been promised something in exchange for hanging out with me? Would you all rather be doing something else?"

"Of course not. I'm having a crackin' time," Gordo said. Then he looked at Caroline. "Although, I don't much care for standing in queues."

Sam licked a finger and tossed me a bag. "I think you know how I feel about shopping and salons. I actually quite prefer the sights." He looked at Caroline. "The queues don't bother me."

Ellie studied her feet.

"Ellie?" I asked.

"I like the sights, and I also like getting my nails done. I liked the zombie picture, and I also liked hearing about Anne Boleyn. Can I just say that I like it all?"

Her indifference clearly annoyed Caroline, who huffed. She sucked in a breath like she was about to explain herself, but I didn't want to hear it.

I stormed out of the salon. When my feet hit the cold sidewalk, I realized that I was barefoot. And I didn't know where to go. My mind raced through the last few days: the whispers when she talked to Stepmummy, making sure I smiled big, agreeing to do stuff that I knew she didn't want to.

I contemplated jumping on a red hop-on, hop-off bus destined for somewhere—anywhere—but I realized I didn't have my new fancy purse either. I wasn't going anywhere except back into that salon.

Maybe the old Jordan would run away, but J.J. wasn't going to, although I really wanted to. I was going to find a way to make this week memorable for Caroline, whether she liked it or not. If being blackmailed by Sebastian and potentially chased by the police wasn't enough, I really didn't know how to take things up a notch on the exciting scale.

"J.J.!" someone yelled. It took me a minute to realize he was talking to me. I turned to see Sam jogging down the street after me. "Hey!" he said. "I think you forgot something. You can't go far without these." He held up my shoes and purse.

I slipped my shoes onto my feet and instantly felt the polish smear. *So much for having pretty toes.*

"Thanks," I said.

"No biggie. But I have something else that might help."

I opened the bag and found a black and white cookie. "Oh, this is so great. Thanks." I wiped a tear out of the corner of my eye. "She's a terrible person, right?"

"If I thought that, I wouldn't hang out with her. I think she's trapped inside the body of someone who started acting like a terrible person a long time ago, and now she can't get away from it. If you notice sometimes, she forgets to put on the act and she's totally normal."

"I thought she liked me when we were at Daphne's. I mean, we had an awesome night."

"Maybe we all pretend to be someone we're not sometimes," he said. "You think Gordo likes going out to watch football and eat wings with me? No, he'd rather be at a museum or reading or something, but he acts like a sports fan when we do that."

I thought about how I was pretending to be someone that I wasn't. "I guess I get that."

"And even though she told Ellie that she was tired of standing in queues, I don't believe it. You can't tell me that she didn't like seeing the Crown Jewels, or the Daphne dresses at Madame Tussauds. She's not that good an actress. That was real." He was still holding my purse. He swung it over his shoulder and pushed out his hip. "How about we skip the rest of the salon activities and make a run to Buck-P."

"Buck-P?"

"Yes, the palace. As in Buckingham," Sam said. "Or we could go to the London Dungeon, but that's really more fun after dark."

The mention of the London Dungeon gave me an

idea, an exciting, fun, and totally un-boring idea that would get even with Caroline for making me feel like a joke. I would play a good one on her. As we walked to the bus stop, I explained it to Sam.

"You're so creative. First you have an idea to nail Sebastian and now a plan to prove to Caroline just how much fun an American exchange student can be?" He picked up his finger-phone. "Can I talk to the man with the plan? Sorry, I meant *woman* with the plan. Oh, never mind. She's right here." He actually said "Click" as he hung up his fingers. "It takes the biscuit."

I was pretty sure that was a biscuit I wanted to take.

Sam knew exactly which bus to get on and led me up the staircase inside. The second floor of the bus was open like a convertible, no roof. Sam chose a seat near the front, and I sat next to him. He handed me a little plastic bag of earphones. "Might as well have some fun on the way," he explained.

Sam opened his bag and plugged the earphones into a hole in the seat in front of us. I did the same and suddenly heard a British voice telling me about the streets we were driving through.

We went through an intersection that the voice said was called Piccadilly Circus, which wasn't a circus at all. It was just an intersection where a bunch of streets came together. *How can they do that? Call it a circus when it isn't?*

Whoever named it had done a really bad job.

We passed the Marble Arch, which is a white marble monument on a large traffic island. A long time ago it stood in front of Buckingham Palace. Historically, only members of the royal family were allowed to pass through the arch in ceremonial processions. But now it's out for everyone. At least that's what the voice in my ears said.

Right before we hopped off the bus at "Buck-P," I noticed an Internet café. I made a mental note about the location because we needed to go there to plant the seeds needed to nail Sebastian. But there was one biggie of a problem with that plan. I needed someone who could build a website.

I crossed the street with a crowd of tourists, and I stood in awe as I stared at the palace. As the queen's official London residence, it was heavily guarded, and was so large that it frightened me. We passed through the golden gates and got closer. It was even bigger up close. I took several pictures, including a handful of the royal guards.

Sam went on a search for food while I thought about my plan for Caroline. It would take place tomorrow night at the London Dungeon.

Tomorrow was going to be a very big day.

22

Sam and I walked into a lobby that looked like it could've been in a grand hotel in Washington DC. The floors were white marble with speckles of gray. The wallpaper was textured velvet. I wanted to touch it, but I figured that was a big no-no.

We followed the tour guide up a set of stairs on one side of the lobby; a matching set of stairs climbed up the other side. They wrapped around toward the center and formed a balcony on the second floor to what the tour guide called a state room.

I stopped to look at a gigantic painting of a ship and the ocean. I wondered if it was one of the ships the explorers had taken as they'd set out in search of the New World. It was really bizarre to think there was a time when people didn't know America existed.

"J.J.?" Sam asked.

"What?"

"The group is leaving us. Come on."

I didn't realize that I'd stopped walking. I glanced behind me for one more glimpse of the painting before catching up with the group. The tour guide described the value of the queen's collection of gowns, many of which had been sewn by Daphne. "Today Daphne's daughter, Sophie, makes clothes for the royal family sometimes, and Daphne's granddaughter, Rose, is learning the family trade. Both Sophie and Rose frequently visit the palace to have tea with the queen, and to fit her gowns."

We stopped at a state room, which looked like a ballroom—a very grand ballroom. It was fit for a queen to entertain guests and host ceremonies. The floor was adorned with an oriental rug; the ceiling was high and carved in elaborate designs. In the front of the room there were three steps leading up to a platform on which two thrones sat—actual real thrones. Behind them was a long heavy red curtain. My parents would love this, so I sent them a picture. Of course, there were tons of security people and one of them was in the picture too. I figured it would help them think I was safe.

At the end of the tour I checked my cell phone messages and found one from Liam. He said he would pick me up whenever I was ready to leave. He said I shouldn't rush. I guess Caroline had told him to fetch me. I needed a chauffeur in Wilmington, Delaware; I really did.

Liam gave the horn a light tap when he saw us among the crowds of tourists lingering in front of the palace. It was a long ride out of the city. We dropped Sam off, and I went back to the manor house. Liam said, "Miss Caroline is home, lying down. She said she left sightseeing early due to a terrible headache." He didn't sound like he believed it. "She explained that Sam was accompanying you. Mr. Gordo and Ellie went home. Mr. and Mrs. Littleton are at a government function tonight, and I made you a shepherd's pie for dinner."

"Thank you, Liam. I'm hungry and tired."

The evening was quiet. Caroline was in her room

and I didn't see her. I was alone for the first time in a few days, and I actually enjoyed the quiet.

Before I went to sleep, I double-checked my plan to pull an awesome and memorable prank on Caroline. It certainly wouldn't be a quiet day tomorrow.

23

The next morning I slept until nine o'clock. I felt well rested for the first time since my arrival in London. It was my second-to-last day in England.

On my way down a massive hallway, I passed Mr. Littleton's home office. It sounded like he was in there. I wanted to introduce myself, but I didn't want to interrupt.

As I debated whether or not to go in, I overheard him talking on the phone. "Daphne's, Incorporated, released its quarterly earnings today. Profits were down for the eighth straight time. Tell the police commissioner that . . ."

The rest was muffled like he was moving around while he talked on the phone.

Interesting. While Daphne's dresses were remarkable, the store was having money problems. I also wondered what Mr. Littleton's job was that he was talking about Daphne's profits and a police commissioner.

Caroline and Mrs. Littleton were in the kitchen sipping tea and flipping through magazines. They sat as far apart at the table as they could possibly be. "Well, good morning, sleepyhead," Mrs. Littleton said. "All the fun catches up with ya, doesn't it?"

"Yes, it did."

I looked at Caroline, who was staring out the window. I could feel the tension between us like I could feel the grumbling in my belly.

"Caroline's headache is all gone, so y'all can have a day filled with sightseeing. Where do you still need to go?"

"I was thinking we would go to the Royal Mews, and tonight I made reservations at the London Dungeon." I swear I saw Caroline's eyes roll back in her head. "I have a feeling it's going to be a very memorable night."

I had an extra bowl of cereal they called muesli. "Are you ready to go to the Mews?"

Caroline said, "It'll probably take a while for the

others to get ready, a few hours at least. Maybe we can go later."

I ignored her and fixed my lipstick. Liam pulled up in the driveway and parked near the front door. He walked around the black car and opened the door for Gordo, Sam, and Ellie.

"What were you saying?" I finally asked Caroline, putting my lipstick back into my purse. She just gave me a dirty look and went off to grab her bag.

Mrs. Littleton said, "Well, I think it's great for you to get an early start on the day." She walked over to her bag, which looked fancy. She took out several bills and handed them to me. "Today is my treat. Y'all go to the Mews, have lunch, and do the Dungeon thingy. This should cover it."

I tried to protest, but she said, "Nonsense. You're our guest, and I haven't treated you to a thing yet. Have fun!" She put her purse away and headed toward the hall. "Just remember to text the pictures." She winked at me.

"No problem," I said, and thanked her. I looked at the bills in my hand. What a normal person would've seen as a few hundred pounds, I saw as my ticket out of spreading poopy fertilizer.

2 4

We took the train into the city. Sam asked me, "Did you tell them your idea to nab Sebastian?"

"What idea?" Caroline asked.

I explained it. "You think it'll work?" I asked.

"Unlikely," Caroline said.

"We need to create a website," Sam said. "Can you do that?" he asked Gordo.

"I guess. People do it all the time," Gordo said. "A few hours at an Internet café, and I could probably figure it out. It can't be rocket science."

"Couple of hours?" Ellie guffawed. "Seriously?"

"I think," Gordo defended himself. "I've never done it before."

"Well," Ellie said, "I have. I could do it in twenty minutes. Piece of cake."

"Did you say *cake*?" Sam asked. "Great. Now I'm hungry."

I asked Ellie, "You know how to create a website?"

"Sure. I have one."

"You have a website?" Caroline asked. "How come you never told us?"

"I didn't think you'd be interested."

"What kind of site?" I asked.

Ellie took the iPad from Sam and touched the screen. "Elly's Inventions and TC Ideas and Stuff."

"What's 'TC'?" I asked.

"'Totally cool,'" she said. "I need to update the name." She tap-tap-tapped, and presto! It read: "Ellie's Inventions and TC Ideas and Stuff."

"I give trendy ideas to people all over the world," Ellie continued. "Where do you think the idea for glow-in-the-dark socks came from? Dyeing white cats purple? All my ideas that are now being done everywhere. A website is powerful."

Sam added, "You are full of surprises."

"I'm officially impressed," Gordo said, and he bowed down to her. As he stood himself back up, he saw the screen in the front of the train. "Check out the telly," Gordo said.

"Top news story today. An attempt has been made on the Crown Jewels," Cole the reporter said.

Skye said, *"Cole, this is major. And I understand there is some connection to the Daphne's heist, is that right?"*

"There is," he said. *"Investigators believe the equipment stolen from Daphne's was used in the attempt. In addition the security cameras at the Tower of London were temporarily redirected so they couldn't capture the robbers' image. However, they missed something."* The telly showed a blurry image.

"Is that one of the ghosts that supposedly live in the Tower? Cole, are you telling us that the spirits tried to steal the Crown Jewels?"

"Although that would be an interesting story, that's not what I'm saying. This is a reflection from one of the mirrors that tell you if someone is approaching from around a corner in the narrow corridors. Seems one of the thieves was unknowingly captured in the mirror's image," Cole said.

Skye asked, *"Do the police think the 'Daphne's Duo,' as the pair of girls in the Internet video are now referred to, are responsible?"*

"The girls are among the suspects in this failed attempt," Cole said.

"So what's next?" Skye asked.

"Video analysts will cross-check visitors from Daphne's with the Tower of London and see who visited both sights over the last few days. We can expect this to be a very long list of suspects, Skye."

"Long indeed. Thanks, Cole."

"That's incredible," Gordo said.

I added, "And we were just there."

25

The Royal Mews were the queen's riding stables and were part of Buck-P. I'm actually not crazy about horses. They scare me a little. I only picked this place because I'd seen the Internet café yesterday.

We walked through the tour of the Mews, which showed us both old and new motor cars and horse-drawn carriages. The horses were often out in the country training and resting, but today they were here in London, so that was kind of a big deal to the people who fancied horses.

As we were leaving, a straight-faced royal guard approached us. "Pardon me."

Regardless of the beret and postage-stamp glasses, I thought for sure we'd been identified from the Internet videos. From the expressions on everyone else's faces, they thought so too.

"Are you Caroline Littleton and company?"

"Nope," Caroline said, looking at her feet.

The guard didn't believe her. "Miss Littleton, your father has arranged a VIP tour for you and your friends."

"VIP?" Ellie asked. "Ha-ha-ha! I said 'pee'!"

"We just finished our tour," Caroline said.

"A trail ride is a unique experience reserved for only very special guests."

"Wait a minute," Gordon said. "Your dad can pull strings with the queen but can't get you a meeting with Daphne's daughter?"

I was still stuck on this VIP thing. "Like, a ride on one of the queen's horses?" I asked. "Shut up!"

The guard looked confused. "That won't be necessary. You can talk whilst you ride. Please follow me."

"Is he serious?" I asked.

"Quite," Caroline said. "You know how to ride, right?"

"Ride a horse? Of course." I let out a little awkward

laugh. "That rhymes." Hopefully I covered up my nervousness.

"Good. Then you won't embarrass me," Caroline said. I figured there was a high possibility that I would embarrass her.

We followed the guard, who delivered us to a stable helper. Gordo walked next to me. "You've never ridden, have you?"

"Shh," I said. "How'd you know?"

"I think you rhyme when you lie."

"I do?"

"Don't worry. I won't tell anyone," he said, and pretended like he was locking his lips.

"What am I gonna do?"

"You don't have many options. I say, 'fess up or fake it'?"

"I think 'fake it,'" I said.

"Me too," Gordo said.

"Stay between me and Sammy. These horses are really well trained. They should just stay in line."

"And if they don't?"

"How far could they go? This place is all fenced in and protected by the royal guard."

I said, "That doesn't make me feel better."

"Just keep your eyes on me. I'll help you."

"Okay."

Sam came over. "Is this totally boss, or what?"

"Saddle or paddle, that's what I always say," I said.

Sam looked from me to Gordo. "Oh, bloody mess. She doesn't know how to ride, does she?"

Sam saw right through me. "I am going to fake it," I said. "Gordo said it will be fine."

"All-righty. Good luck with that," Sam said. "Make sure you tighten your helmet."

We walked to the stables, which were clean, like just-mopped-and-dusted clean. The groom, which is what they called the stable helper, got us on the horses. I was behind Gordo and in front of Sam. I handed the groom my phone and asked her to take a few pictures of us.

After I sent those photos to Mrs. Littleton, we waited to be led to the trail. My horse dug his big nose into anything he saw, while everyone else's stood in line. "Pull up," the groom said, but I didn't know what to pull— my legs, the saddle, the horse's mane. "Pull up," she said again when the horse stuck his snout into a bucket of brushes, knocking it over.

I looked at Gordo, who demonstrated what it

looked like to pull up on the straps that held a very uncomfortable-looking gadget on the horse's face.

Gordo mouthed the word "harder" to me, and I pulled up as hard as I could. This beast was strong, but the tug made him lift his head and stay in line.

The groom and her horse slowly walked out of the stable. The five of us followed. I swayed from side to side on the strong black horse. The ground looked far away, farther than I thought it would when I'd been standing on the ground. I was a little scared, but it wasn't too bad—I could do this, I could totally ride a horse. How hard could this be?

Then the groom kicked her heels into the sides of her horse. It began to trot. Caroline's and Ellie's followed. Gordo kicked his heels, and his horse took off. And mine started to go faster without me even kicking.

Someone yelled, "Ahh!"

When I realized it was me, I tried to stop, but my body jerked with each trot, and with each jerk I couldn't help letting out a grunt. I held the saddle and reins for dear life.

My helmet bopped around on my head until it covered my eyes.

My horse ran faster and my body sagged off the saddle.

My left foot came out of its stirrup as I fell to the right.

I pictured myself falling off and getting trampled to death. Caroline would be beyond embarrassed, but I wouldn't care because I'd be dead, and Ellie would have her fill of blood and guts until the sequel to *Bloodsucking Zombies* was released.

"Gordo!" I called. "Help!" Then, as if the horse could hear me, his stride began to break. The reins felt slightly looser in my hands.

"You're okay," Sam said. He and his horse were very close to me, trotting right by my side.

I moved my helmet out of my eyes.

"That was so freakin' scary," I said, out of breath and almost crying. "You're like a cowboy. How did you know how to do that?"

"I've been around horses since I was little, so it wasn't a big deal. I was watching you closely because I didn't think faking it was gonna work."

"Well, it's a big deal to me. I thought for sure that my insides were going to be stomped out. At least that would take the news coverage away from the videos for a while," I said. "I don't know what I was thinking to believe that I could just hop on and ride a horse. It was a bad idea."

"I'm not going to disagree with you. I should've stopped you."

"Thanks." We approached the stable while the other kids were going down a path. "Did Caroline see?"

Sam and his horse casually led me back to the stables. "Not a thing," he said. "I'm sure."

26

We had to pull Ellie away from the horses. She kept kissing them and thanking them.

"It's their job," Caroline said. "You don't have to thank them."

Gordo said, "Besides, these aren't the talking kind of horses. So they don't understand you anyway." He was teasing her, but I didn't think she knew that.

"Let's go across the street to the Internet café now," I said. That was really where I'd wanted to go all along.

"Yes!" Sam said. "I'm getting a sandwich. Tuna. Possibly with bacon. Maybe soup, too."

Gordo said, "You're going to be a human trash compactor before long."

"That day is not today, Gordo. You want soup too? And maybe we can share a little cheese plate, eh? You wanna?" Sam asked. I think he knew Gordo wouldn't eat soup and a cheese plate.

"Maybe a cup of soup," Gordo said. "*If* it has noodles."

On our way Ellie asked me, "Where do you think they keep the talking horses?"

I said, "I don't think Gordo was serious."

"Why?" Ellie asked. "They probably have to keep them away from the crowds."

And this is the girl who was going to build the website?

At the café we all got soup and sat at a big booth in the corner. Ellie stared at the café-supplied computer. "Now, what exactly do you want me to do?"

I explained my idea. "Create a website that will be a reference in the bibliography. When the teacher checks the site, she'll find our message explaining what Sebastian has done. We'll ask her to *temporarily* give him a B-plus until he returns what he has of ours. She'll e-mail us that she's gotten our message, and we'll reply when it's all clear to give him an F for cheating."

"Why don't we just e-mail the teacher now?" Caroline asked. "In fact, why didn't we do that three days ago and skip writing the paper?"

I said, "Because he would've posted our videos all over the place."

"Right," Ellie said. "I can do this superfast. But how will the teacher know to go to this site?"

I explained, "She'll check the references."

"You think she'll check every single one?" Gordo asked.

"The URL name is going to be important. It will have a subtle clue that the teacher will notice but Sebastian won't. The clue will make her think, 'I better check this one out.'"

"Like what?" Ellie asked.

"Maybe 'www.dwarfplanetpluto.com, "The depressing truth about Pluto," by I. M. Acheater.' Get it?" I added. "Like 'I AM A CHEATER.' The teacher probably knows the Pluto websites that students use for this project, but when she doesn't recognize this one, she'll look it up."

"And when she does," Sam finished, "she'll find our message."

"What if Sebastian decides to check it out too?"

Caroline asked. "He's a twerp, not an idiot."

"Too true," Ellie said. "It could totally backfire on us, in which case your late-night videos will be Internet sensations and you'll be in the tank for grand theft."

Caroline yelled, "We didn't steal anything!"

Ellie added, "It's your word against theirs."

"WHO!" Caroline yelled. "Who is 'they'?" She seemed frustrated with Ellie.

Ellie said, "You know, the popo, the police!"

Sam asked Caroline, "Are the police going to believe you? I mean, you *were* in the store the night the stuff was stolen."

Gordo pushed his unfinished soup cup aside and nibbled his baguette. "I don't think this is gonna work."

Sam took the soup cup and drained it into his mouth. "Bummer." He wiped the corner of his mouth on a cloth napkin. "It sounded like a good idea."

"It can still work," Ellie said.

We listened to her idea. There was a 50 percent chance it would involve talking horses and a 50 percent chance it would be brilliant. "We'll hold the bibliography until right before the paper is due and make him meet with us in order to get it. We can meet him at Lively's tomorrow morning and exchange the bib for the flash drive with the videos. That way he won't have time to check the references."

Caroline asked, "And what if he doesn't like this idea and he blasts more evidence of us at Daphne's? The next batch might include our faces."

"If he did that, he wouldn't get his bibliography, and without that he won't get a B-plus," Ellie said.

We all looked at her.

"Why are you all staring at me?" she asked. "I think it'll work."

"It will," I said. "You're a tiara-wearing-glow-in-the-dark-sock-and-zombie-loving genius."

"Thanks. Give me a half hour. It will be a bomb-diggity," Ellie said with a proud smile.

We watched every tap she made on the computer. She stopped and peered up at us. "I can't work under this pressure. Why don't you go shopping or something?"

Caroline said, "You don't have to ask me twice." She tossed her purse over her shoulder, flipped on her white rhinestone sunglasses, and tucked her hair back into the red beret.

"Ditto," Gordo said. The two of them left, arms hooked together.

Sam and I moved to a different table. "Wanna share a piece of pie?" I asked.

He said, "I don't know. Let me think. Do I want pie? Am I even hungry? Oh, this is a hard decision. Maybe I should call the DUH, YES, I LOVE PIE ASSOCIATION."

"Funny," I said. "I'll get it." I returned with one plate and two forks.

"Think it'll work?" I asked.

"I think it just might," he said.

"Done," Ellie announced. "Easy peasy." She left the booth where she'd been working and came to sit with us, picking up a fork from another table on her way. She took a wee teeny bite of pie. "Oh. That is so good, I could have another bite." She took another teensy-weensy bite, and said, "Yup. Still good."

"Since that's done, I can tell you my secret plans for tonight," I told Ellie. "I'm going to need your help to make this a night Caroline will never forget."

She dropped the fork and slapped her hands over her ears. "La-la-la. If it's a secret, don't tell me. I'm terrible at keeping secrets. I don't mean to be; I just can't remember what's secret and what's not. So, don't tell me. I trust you guys. Let's just assume I love the idea and it will be a great night."

"Okay. I won't tell you."

Ellie dropped her hands and continued to take itsy-bitsy bites of the pie, until it was gone.

Sam didn't stop her but watched with surprise.

Then Ellie rummaged through her purse for a lip gloss and applied. When she was done, she looked at the plate. "Oh my, Sam, it's all gone." I don't think she realized she'd eaten the whole thing.

"It's all right," Sam said. "I wasn't hungry anyway."

27

On our way to the train, we passed a store where Caroline "had to" stop. She and Ellie went in while Sam and Gordo searched for a loo.

"I'll wait here," I said. "And look in the windows."

I strolled about half a block, to where I stumbled on Lively's main location. Immediately I knew I wanted to get Sam a lemon tart since Ellie had eaten all the pie.

Sebastian was behind the bakery counter taking muffins out of a pan. "Oh, look what the wind blew in," he said to himself but loud enough for me to hear. "Where is the rest of your mob?"

"Shopping."

"How come you're not with them?"

"I wanted a snack."

He placed the pan down and picked up another. "Oh, bloody blast it!" He dropped the pan. It made a loud *klunk-klank* on the ground. He held out his hand. "Wonkers! That was hot."

I marched right behind the counter to see the burn. "Come to the sink." I turned the knob of a big stainless steel sink and guided his burned hand under the faucet.

"Ah, that feels good," he said.

"Do you have ice?"

"In that chest." His eyes directed me to a giant freezer that opened like an army trunk. I broke off a chunk of ice. "Grab some butter, too, will you?"

"Ice. I read that ice is better for a burn than butter." I wrapped the ice in a paper towel, guided his hand out of the water, and set the towel on the red spot. "How does that feel?"

"Not bad. Not good, either, but not bad." He looked at me. "Thanks. My mum has ointment in the back. I'll put that on and bandage it." Sebastian went into the back of the store, and I lost sight of him.

"Hello?" a voice called to me from the customer side of the counter. I looked at a woman in a purple pantsuit and facial wrinkles down to her elbows. She said, "I'll have a prune Danish and tea."

"I . . . ummm, errr . . ."

"Two lumps of sugar in the tea, dear."

"Two?" I put what I was pretty sure was a prune Danish on a plate, and tipped some hot tea into a dainty cup. I looked around for sugar, found a canister, and plopped in two lumps. I put the plate and cup on the counter, but the lady was gone. She had sat herself down and was tucking her legs under a table.

I brought the items to her.

"Oh, thank you. You are so sweet."

Sebastian still hadn't returned. I went back to the scene of the burn, scooped the broken bits of blueberry muffins off the floor, and put them into the trash. I found a broom and was sweeping when Sebastian appeared with a bandage on his hand. His eyes widened when he looked at me cleaning.

"You're cleaning up my mess?"

"I was just helping." I thought maybe he was mad. "And that lady. She wanted a Danish—"

"You served Mrs. Sawyer?"

"I guess so."

"Why are you trying to be so nice to me? Do you want something? Did Caroline send you here?"

"I'm not *trying* to be nice. I *am* nice."

Sebastian seemed to accept this explanation as he sent me on my way with two free tarts.

But was I nice? I'd just made sure he'd get an F.

28

The London Dungeon lived up to its name. The outside was lit with medieval torches. The building was windowless and gray. Standing outside the bleak and dreary attraction, Ellie said, "Thank you! Thank you, J.J., for bringing us here. This is like a real live horror movie that we are going to go in. I swear life can't get better than this."

The London Dungeon was a cross between a haunted house, an amusement park ride, and a history lesson. It was like walking, or riding, through London's haunted history, which was presented with elaborate scenes and live actors that tried to scare you.

I looked at Caroline, who let out a yawn, which she covered with her fist. *You better get your yawns in now,* I thought. *Someone might get a little extra scared tonight.*

Sam looked at his phone. "Okay. I just sent Sebastian the last pages except for the bibliography. I told him we'll meet him tomorrow morning at Daphne's at nine o'clock and trade it for the flash drive."

Everything for Sebastian was ready. And we were on the cusp of entering what could've been hell.

A bald man dressed in a black gown like an executioner directed us to enter the damp dungeon.

Ellie said, "The best night EVER!" And she jumped around.

Inside was like a dark, scary cave. We walked a narrow path and looked at the horrible scenes in each crevice. They were disgusting displays with actors in very realistic costumes being executed, tortured, and locked in stockades and cages. It was truly horrific. Sometimes someone would jump out at us and try to catch us to bring us into their deadly world.

The medieval times were gruesome and barbaric. I'd been in London for four days, and I'd been so busy transforming myself, taking pictures and videos, writing a paper about Pluto, hiding from the police, shopping, setting a trap for Sebastian, *and* planning this charade for Caroline that I hadn't noticed the obvious—this place was superold, older than anything in the US. They had way more history all around them than we could ever have. That was the history I'd come here to see.

I could hear the sound of water as we progressed through the cavernous halls.

A woman dressed in rags screamed in my face, "Get in the boat! Hurry!" Fake blood dripped down her face and stuck in her matted hair. I stepped into the boat. The flat-bottom was filled with about an inch of water that soaked right through my sneakers. The boat wobbled from side to side, and I thought for a second I might go overboard. We all made it onto the craft and sat real close together on two rows of bench seats that didn't feel strong or sturdy under my butt.

Ellie was giddy with excitement. She still didn't know the plan, so I whispered into her double-pierced ear, "Whatever happens, just go with it. It's all part of the secret plan that I didn't tell you."

"Got it."

The boat floated down the indoor river toward fog and screams. It got darker, and Ellie said, "I think I just tinkled."

Gordo, who was sitting next to her, said, "No, baby doll. I think that was me."

The boat disappeared into the tunnel. The actors around us screamed in pain. One guy with a huge zipper scar on his face tried to climb into the boat with us, but Sam pushed him away. I heard Gordo let out a blood-curdling howl, then shout, "Get off me! Get away! Ahhh!"

"What's the matter?" Caroline asked.

It was all part of the plan.

Sam yelled like someone had cut off his arms or taken away his last cupcake. "No! No! Oh my God!"

I joined in with my own shouts of terror.

Caroline frantically asked questions, "What's the matter? What's going on? Ellie, where are you?"

No one answered, because we all snuck out of the boat and left Caroline all alone.

"Gordo? J.J.?" She was crying now. "What's happening?"

From our hiding place I saw the boat float past a scene of King Henry's daughter, who was known as Bloody Mary.

The boat came out of the tunnel to where candles hung on the walls. I saw Caroline looking around her and realizing that she was alone. All alone in the horrible cavern. She called to the ghoulish actors, "Help me! My friends are gone! They've been taken." But they ignored her and continued on with their show.

I laughed so hard that I thought that *I* might tinkle. We walked along a narrow and ghoul-less path to get to the end of the ride before Caroline, and we hid in the darkness.

At last the boat bumped the edge of a dock. Caroline jumped out. She looked at the empty boat and screamed to everyone, "Call the police. Oh my God! Oh my God, they're all gone."

We let her go a minute longer before coming out from the shadows. We all burst out in laughter. It was we-totally-got-you-with-this-joke laughter.

There was no way she could EVER forget this night.

29

Caroline didn't think the joke was as funny as the rest of us did. Even the actors and people who worked at the London Dungeon thought it was hysterical.

"Why would you do this?" she asked Sam and Gordo.

"J.J. set it up," Gordo said.

Sam said, "It was priceless." He held his hand up for a high five. "Up top." I smacked it.

"You?" she asked me, moving very close to my face. "Why?"

"You said this was a boring week," I said. "The only

reason you were nice to me was so that you could go on a vacation. Now the joke's on you."

She pursed her lips and held in whatever it was she wanted to say as we made our way to the train.

As with every other train ride, the telly was on in the front of the car. Once again the news involved us.

"It's unbelievable, Skye. Another robbery. This one was quite successful. Two famous Daphne dresses were stolen last night from Madame Tussauds."

"Last night, Cole?" Skye asked. "Why are we just hearing about this now?"

"The blue and red dresses were replaced with imitations. The swap wasn't discovered until midday. Oh, and guess where the fake dresses came from?"

"I'm gonna say the Dress-Up Department of Daphne's. Looks like it was the Daphne's Duo again."

"Actually," Cole said, "authorities think the real mastermind might have uploaded videos of the duo just to throw investigators off his or her scent."

"It did, indeed," Skye said.

"Now the police are looking for the source of the uploaded videos with hopes that it will lead to the true mastermind behind this recent string of robberies."

"Do you know what that means?" Gordo asked.

"They think Sebastian is the real mastermind," we all said, and had a gut-busting laugh.

"Do you think the police will actually look for him?" I asked.

"Who cares?" Caroline asked. "Let the little poop get in trouble. Uploading those videos without our permission is probably illegal somewhere."

"If it's not, it should be," Gordo agreed. Then he asked, "Do you think it's strange that we've been to all three of the places where there have been crimes?"

"They're three of the most popular tourist attractions in England," Sam said.

"Well, I think that is smashing news," Ellie said.

Sam asked, "That they think it's Sebastian?"

"That they think it's anyone other than the Daphne's Duo here." Ellie indicated Caroline and me. "I gotta be honest, I thought it was you guys all along."

30

We huddled under umbrellas outside Daphne's at 8:55 the next morning. It wasn't raining hard but spitting enough to return the curl to my flat-ironed hair, which I'd pulled back into a braid. I'd ditched the crocheted cap, and Caroline had lost her beret.

At precisely nine the doors opened and we raced to Lively's. Sebastian wasn't there. The lady behind the counter introduced herself as his mom. I was dying to tell her what Sebastian had been up to. Sam, on the other hand, took advantage of the situation and ordered lemon tarts without spit. Mrs. Lively was so nice, she didn't even charge him.

"How did Sebastian get to be such a creep?" I asked Sam. "His mom seems very kind."

"Dunno."

Mrs. Lively said, "I called Sebastian to tell him that his friends were here looking for him. He said he was on his way."

"Pardon me, Mrs. Lively," Ellie said. "I see you have a computer there." She indicated behind the counter. "I'm looking for a grade from my teacher. Would you mind if I checked my school account really quick? I'm so nervous about this grade."

"Well, I suppose that would be okay. I understand how important your grades are," she said. "You know, Sebastian is handing in a critical paper today. His scholarship depends on it. You help yourself." She placed a glass of juice on the counter for each of us. We hadn't even asked for them.

Ellie walked behind the counter.

"What do you mean about his scholarship?" Sam asked Mrs. Lively.

"Sebastian has to keep a B-plus average or he'll lose the scholarship he needs to attend your school."

"Oh." Sam tugged me, Gordo, and Caroline away

from Mrs. Lively. "If Sebastian gets caught cheating, or gets an F, he'll lose his scholarship."

"He's a cheater," Caroline said. "He deserves to fail and to lose his scholarship."

"If everyone got what they deserved, you'd be locked up somewhere for spending the night at Daphne's," Sam said.

"You know that was way different. I'm not a jerk and a blackmailer," she said.

Gordo said, "Sebastian and I used to be science lab partners. He was fine until you started talking rubbish about him."

"Are you joshing me? He's evil," she said. "You're just gonna have to trust me on that."

No one said anything. It seemed like Caroline's friends weren't willing to "just trust" her the way they used to or the way she wanted.

Ellie came out from behind the counter.

"What was that about?" I asked her.

"I asked myself, if I was Sebastian, would I just hand over all my videos to you guys?"

Gordo asked, "And what did you answer yourself?"

"No. I would make a copy."

Sam said, "Which you just found."

"I did. And I replaced it with this." She pointed to

her phone's screen. There was a video of Ellie. Her hands were in front of her mouth and she pretended she was playing a clarinet. "Hmm doot doot doo."

"What's this?" Sam asked her.

"It's that new Mash-Up song played on an invisible clarinet. Can't you tell?"

Gordo said, "That doesn't sound like Mash-Up at all."

Sam ignored the insignificant debate. "What did you do?"

"I replaced the video of Caroline and J.J. with their bums in the pastry case with this," she said. "I left the old file name so he'll think he still has it, but he has Invisible Clarinet instead." Then she added, "BTW, in the cloud he has another folder called 'Caroline Heart.'"

"Ooh, someone has a crush," Gordo said.

"Heart?" Caroline asked. "I think I just barfed in my mouth."

Gordo started a slow, steady clap. We all joined in. She smiled a huge yes-I-know-I-am-awesome smile.

"He can't get us now. We're free," Caroline said.

Sebastian came into the Hall of Gourmets, nearly a half hour late.

"You're late," Caroline said. "I guess you're not too worried about having that paper in by ten o'clock."

"Patience, Cruella," he said. "It's actually not due until eleven. I just wanted you to wait for me."

"You're a real creep," Caroline said.

"And you're a snob," Sebastian said back.

"Oh, blast!" I yelled, using my new British expression. I'd spilled my juice down the front of my shirt. Everyone looked at me. "Sebastian, can you show me the sink, please?"

He huffed like it was terribly inconvenient, then led me to their kitchen and to the sink. I turned on the water, and he was about to walk away. "Wait," I said. "Remember when I said I was nice?"

He nodded.

"Well, I did something not very nice." He listened. "You're gonna get an F as soon as you hand over the flash drive. And then you'll lose your scholarship."

"No I won't. I have insurance."

"Not anymore." His forehead creased in the center. "Turns out Ellie is a computer wiz. Your insurance is gone." His face turned a dark shade of red.

He smashed his fist into his hand. "I'll still get them." His evil mind looked like it was racing for a new plan.

"How about you don't?"

"What do you mean?" he asked.

"Take the B-plus. Keep your scholarship."

"You said you made it so I would get an F."

"I can undo that." I hoped I could. "And when I do, let's just drop this, okay?"

He thought and picked at the bandage on his burn. "What's in it for me?"

"Seriously? You get to stay in school, keep your scholarship, and get a B-plus on a paper that you didn't even write."

He picked some more.

Sam handed Sebastian a small red flash drive. "Now hand over the flash drive."

Sebastian took it out of his pocket. "Here you go. One worm chock-full of incriminating videos and pictures. It's all yours."

Caroline took the worm and squeezed it in her fist.

Sebastian disappeared behind the pastry counter, but not before glancing at me.

"We should check it," Sam said. "Make sure it's the right worm." He put it into the iPad and started watching the video of us dancing around in costumes. "You two had quite a busy night."

"Then our mission is complete," Caroline said. "By this time tomorrow he'll be tossed from school."

I felt sick to my stomach. I knew he cheated, but jeez, this was extreme. "Wait," I said. "We can't let him get kicked out of school."

Caroline said, "Yes we can. We have the flash drive. Let's just go."

I pushed some more. "This isn't worth him losing his scholarship over."

"You don't know him like we do. He's wicked. Now let's get out of here and do something fun. J.J., apparently you're the Queen of Fun. What do you have up your sleeve today?" She didn't sound like she really thought I was the queen of anything.

I asked Ellie, "Is there anything you can do?"

Caroline said, "I said we're leaving it."

"No," I stated firmly. "We're not going to make him lose his scholarship."

She narrowed her eyes into little slits. "What did you say?"

I wanted someone else to say something, but no one did. My heart was racing. I felt sweat in my palms and armpits as Caroline continued to drill me with her nasty stare. "Ellie, what can you do?" I asked.

"Jeez, I perform a few computer miracles, and now you guys think I'm some kind of fairy godmum. Oh, let me wave my wand and—Poof!—it's all good now."

"What about changing his grade in the school computer?" I asked.

"I have ethical standards, and that crosses the line."

"You can do that?" Sam asked.

"Maybe I can, but I don't. If I did, I would've changed your science midterm. You mixed up meiosis and mitosis. I mean, come on, Sam, use your head!"

"What? How did you know I missed those questions?" Sam asked.

"I might snoop from time to time. But that's not important. What we're talking about is where I draw the line. No grade changing."

Sam shook the confusion out of his head. "You are one weird chick."

"Gimme the iPad," I said, and I handed it to Ellie. "Can you make our URL actually go to the real article, so it's all fine?"

Ellie thought for a second, tapped the screen a few times, and said "Uh-huh." Then she handed the tablet back to me. "There you go. Just like you wanted. Fixed," Ellie said. "Now, does anyone want me to change a pumpkin into a carriage?"

"So it's all good, then," I said. I looked at Caroline,

who I knew disapproved of everything I had done. I tried to lighten the mood. "I mean, besides the grossness of Sebastian's crush, of course. That's not good."

There was an awkward pause of quietness.

"Well," Caroline finally said. I was sure her next words would be harsh and hurtful. I squared my shoulders and prepared for the blow. "It's done, then." She un-narrowed her eyes. "I didn't think you had it in you, J.J."

I waited. The lashing was coming; I just knew it. I saw Ellie cringe as she waited for it too. "I expected you to be more of a slug. But you've proven me wrong."

Wait, what just happened?

Gordo studied Caroline with great suspicion in his face. "Who are you, and what have you done with Caroline?"

"Oh, shove off," she said.

He raised his eyebrows. "It's Caroline."

"This is one of those unusual times when things didn't pan out like I'd planned. I didn't mean for you to overhear me at the nail salon, but it was the truth." She continued. "My stepmum bribed me to hang out with you because I didn't want to. I don't really like hanging out with new people. I like my life exactly the way it is. I wasn't interested in prancing around London from sight to sight entertaining a stranger during my week off from school."

Well, at least she was honest. I hadn't really considered that my arrival might have botched up her week.

"Your mom called, and my stepmum said yes, and the rest was on me. No one even asked me if I wanted to be your hostess and tour guide."

I hadn't even thought that she wouldn't be psyched about our week. "So you were promised a trip to Jamaica in exchange for schlepping me around?"

She nodded. "Not a bad deal, eh?"

"I guess."

"What I didn't say at the salon, and maybe I should've, is that I've kinda liked it. I mean, I've lived in this city all my life and I never knew there was a wax figure of my favorite person at Madame Tussauds," she said.

"And the truth is that the whole London Dungeon thing was . . ."

It was coming now. I was going to get a full verbal assault.

"It was freakin' amazing! I mean, I *totally* believed that you had been slashed. I'll be talking about that forever. And the night at Daphne's was pretty awesome." She tossed her beautiful blond hair over her shoulder and put on her big white sunglasses. "I suppose I should thank you."

"You want to thank *me*?"

"Yes. I just did," she said, and rummaged through her purse for her mobile, probably to see who had texted in the last hour. "Should we get going to the abbey, then?"

"Bril," I agreed. Things with Caroline felt good, and I was glad Sebastian would keep his scholarship.

31

The day was dreary and rainy. Everyone was fine with heading home early. Even me. I had to admit that I was exhausted. And maybe I was a little depressed that this would be my last night in Caroline's house, which was like a palace to me.

"It feels good to have all of the Sebastian stuff over with," Ellie said.

Caroline said, "And since the police think our video was just a diversion from the real thief, I feel like I can watch the telly without cringing."

"But the real thief is still out there," Sam said.

"Speaking of the telly, look," Sam said. "It's Skye and Cole with the news."

"This just in. A priceless painting was stolen from Buckingham Palace," said Skye. She showed a shot of the painting. It was the one of the boat.

"Let me guess," Cole said. *"The tools used for this heist were the ones stolen from Daphne's."*

"You got it."

"Do the police have any leads on the robber or robbers?"

"As you know, they have been cross-checking the surveillance footage from all the sights: Daphne's, the Tower of London, Madame Tussauds, and now Buckingham Palace, and they've narrowed down the potential suspects," Skye said.

"That is wonderful news. What about the mirror image from the Tower of London?" Cole asked.

"As soon as it's released, you'll see it here," replied Skye.

"I kinda hoped they'd figure out who it was before I went home," I said. "But I'm just glad they don't really think it was the Daphne's Duo."

"You're going home with a cool story to tell," Gordo

said. "Being suspected of trying to steal the Crown Jewels? It doesn't get any more exciting than that."

"Too true," I agreed.

It was dark when Liam woke me. "Miss J.J., it's time to get ready to go to the airport."

I packed my things and was filled with a satisfaction that I had done what I came for, plus so much more. I'd had a major adventure that I'd never forget, I felt totally un-boring, and most importantly, I'd made four new friends.

I figured I could google the UK news from home to see updates on the crime spree that had plagued London since my arrival.

I brought my things to the living room, where Mrs. Littleton was in front of a seventy-two-inch TV screen, twisting her body in a yoga pose.

"Liam is gonna take you to Heathrow. Gimme a hug now."

I did, and I thanked her for everything.

In the grand marble foyer of the mansion, Caroline waited with a suitcase of her own. "Are you coming with me to Delaware?"

She rolled her eyes. "No. It's a gift." She pushed a case

with a pretty floral pattern on it and the word LONDON written across the top.

"Oh, thank you," I said. I pulled it by its handle. "Why is it so heavy?"

"I might've filled it with the stuff you wanted but didn't buy from Daphne's."

"Are you serious? That's amazing. I love, love, love it." I smiled. "Thank you so much."

I walked out the front door of the fantastic manor house and turned to take another look at it. I wanted to remember all the details. I hoped that someday I would visit this house again.

Liam held the car door open for me. I would have to get used to not having a driver back home.

Ellie, Sam, and Gordo were in the car. "Hi, guys! You all came to say good-bye?"

"Of course," they said in unison.

And off we went to the airport.

At the terminal we said good-bye. "I'll text you," I said to Caroline.

"Of course you will," she said, like I would be so fortunate to text Caroline Littleton, but I knew what she really meant was "I can't wait."

"All right, baby doll. You stay cool," Gordo said.

"I will."

"Seriously, it's been a totally epic week," he said. "You are one of the most interesting and fun people I've ever met."

Ellie was tearing up.

"Ellie," I said. "It'll be okay."

"I'm just going to miss you so much."

"We'll be friends on Facebook so we can always see what the other is doing," I said.

I knew Ellie and I were going to be friends forever.

Sam took my hand. "I wish it had been longer than a week," he said.

"Me too."

A boarding call for my flight bellowed overhead.

"You have to go," he said. He picked up his finger-phone and mouthed the words, "Call me."

"I will." With a wave I headed home with my over-priced purse, a bag full of new clothes, and a new attitude.

3 2

I spread out in my seat, which I found out Mr. Littleton had upgraded to first class for me as a special treat. Have you ever sat in first class? It's *very* nice, like reclining-seat-my-own-TV-phone-WiFi-slippers nice.

I clicked picture after picture of my trip and arranged them in the order I wanted. I typed captions under each, describing Anne Boleyn and showing the yeomen who guard the tower in their uniforms.

As I was going through, I noticed something strange about one yeoman in the photo. I paused for a second, then moved on to the Crown Jewels. Then I explained a bit about Madame Tussauds' history and showed pictures of some current celebrities whose likenesses were frozen in wax, adding more captions along the way. I also added the pictures of the cast of *Bloodsucking Zombies*.

Right before I moved off to the next photo, my eye caught the face of a man in the background. To anyone else he would just look like another tourist, but I recognized this man. It was the same man who had been in the yeoman's uniform, or maybe it wasn't a uniform at all; it was a COSTUME.

I combed through the rest of my photos, carefully looking for the man in the other pictures. And finally, near the end of the album, I found him—a.k.a. Hamlet, the night security guard at Daphne's—at Buckingham Palace dressed as a royal guard, another costume from Daphne's Dress-Up Department.

I pulled out the air phone from the seat in front of me, and I took out my credit card. This *was* an emergency. I dialed a number I'd had in my wallet in case I ever needed it while I was in London. I needed to call Mr. Littleton now.

"It's Jordan Jacoby," I said. "I know who the thief is, and I have proof, photographic proof. I'm sending it to

211

you right now." I paused. "Did you get it? Do you see what I'm talking about? That's the night security guard from Daphne's. His name is Hamlet."

I landed in Philadelphia. After navigating Customs like the experienced international flyer that I was, I was met by a man in a black pin-striped suit and a red tie.

"Excuse me," he said with a British accent that I didn't expect in Philadelphia. "I'm Mark Salyers, the British ambassador. Mr. Littleton sent me. He's very appreciative of your help. Can we talk for a minute?"

"Um, okay," I said.

"Follow me."

I spent the next hour with Ambassador Salyers.

By the time I got home, it was already on the news. Hamlet was in custody. My allegations were confirmed with his image clearly reflected in the mirror at the Tower of London. And the local reporter said that I, J.J. Jordan Jacoby, was offered the gratitude of Her Majesty.

The ambassador had been very kind to me. He said I was welcome in England anytime, and he personally arranged for me to have VIP access to any of the city's sights and palaces. This meant that I didn't need to buy tickets or wait in the queue.

• • •

On Monday at school I gave my presentation in a new outfit from Caroline. I'd put the presentation in a really neat web-based program that Ellie had taught me to use.

I started, "While the Royal Mews are the official stables for the queen . . ." I was in the middle of a pretty good presentation when my mobile . . . err . . . cell phone rang. Whoops.

"I am so sorry. This phone is still new. I thought I'd turned it off," I said to my teacher, embarrassed.

When I glanced down at the phone, I almost hit the floor.

The caller ID said SOPHIA WHITWORTH.

SIX MONTHS LATER

"Top story today is about everyone's favorite store, Daphne's," Skye said.

"Indeed it is, Skye," Cole said. "To increase its business the store has decided to stay open all night long for what it's calling Pillow Parties."

"That's brilliant, Cole. I know I want to go. Do you know who the mastermind was behind this idea?"

"Tell me, Skye," Cole said.

"An American girl named J.J. This is the same girl responsible for identifying the perpetrator behind a rash of thefts that plagued some of our most beloved landmarks just a few short months ago. She is truly an amazing young woman," Skye said.

"Let's show a clip of J.J. and her friends with Sophia and Rose Whitworth at a ribbon-cutting ceremony for the new Slumber Party Department."

Turn the page for a sneak peek at:

Lucky Me

Cindy
Callaghan

Can Meghan turn her luck around?

by Cindy Callaghan

If I had to pick one thing that I believe in more than anything else, it would be this: LUCK. I'm Meghan McGlinchey, the most superstitious thirteen-year-old girl in Delaware, and possibly the world.

For example, I never got out of bed when my digital clock read an odd number. Odd number = bad luck.

7:02. Perfect.

I dressed in a snap because every day it was the same school uniform—boring plaid skirt, plain white shirt, itchy button-up navy-blue sweater, matching headband, horrendous blue leather shoes, and kneesocks. The outfit was—how should I say this?—ugly!

I dashed down the stairs, especially careful to skip the thirteenth step today because it was a very important day, one I'd been looking forward to for weeks. I was running for eighth-grade class president. And today was the election. I had done a stellar job campaigning FOREVER. If I didn't totally mess up my speech, I was pretty sure I was gonna win. With all the practicing I'd been doing, it would take a major freak of nature for me to mess up this speech.

I passed my four sisters and parents scrambling around in the kitchen. I opened a can of food for my cat, Lucky. He ran over when he heard it pop. I scratched his ears as he lapped up the food.

I loved Lucky, but he and I had a problem. He was a black cat. And people like me, we don't mix well with black cats. But we had an understanding: He didn't cross my path, and I took good care of him. It worked for us.

The kitchen was louder than usual this morning. My younger sister Piper (the fifth grader) yelled at one of my older sisters, Eryn (the eleventh grader), "Why did you touch my playlist? Why? WHY?"

Dad yelled across the kitchen to my mom, "Can you put a bagel in the toaster for me?"

The baby cried while my oldest sister sang her an Irish lullaby to calm her. It wasn't working, so she tried some applesauce, which the baby threw across the room. It nearly hit my white shirt, but I ducked out of the way just in time. *SPLAT!* The applesauce hit the wall behind me. *Phew, that was lucky!*

I stood at the front door, under the horseshoe mounted on the wall and next to my lucky snow globe collection, watching the insanity.

The living room was a mess with suitcases and duffel bags. We were leaving the next morning for Ireland, where we would spend spring break. The purpose of the trip was for my father to meet his newly discovered sister. You see, he'd been born in Ireland. Sadly, something had happened to his parents when he was just a kid, and he'd been raised at a home for boys.

Until a few months ago he hadn't thought he had any family. But thanks to some online research, he'd found a long-lost sister. I imagined that when he met her, he'd introduce me as his middle daughter and president of Wilmington Prep's eighth-grade class. It was gonna be totally impressive.

I crunched the granola bar I'd packed in my backpack the night before—instant breakfast. With a little planning my morning was the way I liked it: mayhem-free.

In fact, I liked most things organized. I might have been the most organized eighth grader at Wilmington Prep, an all-girls private school that went from kindergarten through twelfth grade. This meant that Piper and Eryn were in my school. If you knew either Piper or Eryn, you'd know this wasn't a good thing. (Piper was known as the bigmouth, while Eryn was quiet and filled with a bad attitude. I'd heard a lot of nicknames for her, most made up by my bestie, Carissa. None of them were nice.)

While I waited for someone to realize it was time to leave, I flipped through a Forever 21 catalog.

"Meghan," Mom called through the chaos, "you have a letter on the table."

"A letter?" I asked.

"Yes," she said. "You know, the regular old-fashioned paper kind that's delivered by a mailman."

I stepped around the chaos. Sure enough, on the hall table was a letter addressed to *moi*.

Who writes letters anymore when you can just text or e-mail?

The postmark on the envelope said Limerick, Ireland. *Hmmm.*

Dear Friend,

I am starting this chain letter and mailing it to three people to whom I would like to send good luck. In turn they must send it to three people. If you are receiving this, someone has sent the luck to you—as long as you, in turn, send it to three more people within six days.

Chain letters have existed for centuries, and many have traveled around the world. A United States police officer received $25,000 within one day of sending his letters. However, another woman ignored it and lost her life's fortune because she broke the chain. A Norwegian fisherman thought for sure he would never find true love, but just two days after sending his letters, he met the woman of his dreams.

To get your luck and avoid the unlucky consequences, you must:

• Copy this letter

• Add your name below and remove the name above yours

• Mail it to three people within <u>six</u> days

From,

Clare Gallagher, Ireland _____

_____

Clare Gallagher?

I didn't know anyone by that name. *How does she know me?* That wasn't important now. What *was* important was that I send this letter to three people ASAP. No, double-ASAP. Maybe I could get the good luck as soon as today—for the election—and avoid those "unlucky consequences."

I went into my mom and dad's home office and rummaged around.

"What are you doing in there?" Mom called over the havoc.

"Looking for envelopes!"

"I don't have any," Mom said. "Sorry. I'll bring a few home from work tonight."

That would be too late. Maybe I could get a couple from the school office. I only needed three. "How about stamps?"

"Sorry. The baby used them as stickers. I can buy more after vacation."

After vacation wasn't *today*, and I needed the luck *today*.

Eryn bumped me out of her way, causing me to drop the letter. "Move it, buttmunch," she said. She stepped on the letter as she left the house. (This is what I meant about her attitude—bad.)

Piper did pretty much the same thing on her way out, not because she had attitude issues but because she wasn't paying attention.

Shannon picked the letter up for me. She was twenty-two years old and definitely the nicest of my sisters. She commuted to the University of Delaware and itched to finish school so she could move out of our house and "find herself," whatever that meant.

I took the letter, followed Shannon into the car, and climbed in the back with Piper. Eryn sat shotgun. Always. I didn't even try to beat her to the front seat anymore. Shannon always dropped us off at Wilmington Prep, then headed to UD. She picked us up later, on her way home. After school, we did homework or whatever until Mom or Dad got home from the law firm, where they worked together. They were always home for a late full-family dinner, when we talked about our day whether we wanted to or not.

On our drive Piper chattered about our spring break trip, while I just stared out the window.

"What do you guys know about chain letters?" I asked.

Shannon said, "You need to send 'em right away, don't you?"

I could feel Eryn rolling her eyes.

Piper asked a hundred questions: "What's a chain letter? . . . Who sent it? . . . Why? Can you send it back? . . . Why not? How come I didn't get one? . . . Huh?"

I didn't answer her; I responded to Shannon. "I don't have any stamps or envelopes, and I want the good luck today."

"Why don't you e-mail it?" Shannon asked. "You could do that right now on your phone."

Piper said, "Problem solved. Shannon is super-smart. . . ." She continued to ramble on while I typed the letter quickly with my thumbs. I reread it to make sure I hadn't made any mistakes. I put my name on the bottom and removed Clare's. When I finished, Piper was still talking. "She gets As in college. That's a lot of hard work."

I hit the send button on my phone, and e-mail chain letters went out to three friends from summer camp. "Okay. It's done. Let the good luck begin!"

Eryn snickered.

"What?" I asked.

"Oh, nothing," she said with a smirk. "Let me know how that works for you. On second thought, don't. That would mean you'd be talking to me." She made a grossed-out face that I caught in the side mirror. "But any moron knows that you can't e-mail a snail-mail chain letter. It's cheating. And chain letters have a way of messing with cheaters."

Piper said, "Uh-oh."

Uh-oh?

I couldn't have any *uh-oh*.

Not today.

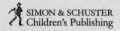

IF YOU ♥ THIS BOOK,

you'll love all the rest from

aladdin m!x™

YOUR HOME AWAY FROM HOME:

AladdinMix.com

HERE YOU'LL GET:

- ♥ The first look at new releases
- ♥ Chapter excerpts from all the Aladdin M!X books
- ♥ Videos of your fave authors being interviewed